BACKROOM BOY

ALL-AMERICAN BOY NOVELLA

MARIKA RAY

MARIKA RAY PUBLISHING

BACKROOM BOY
ALL-AMERICAN BOY NOVELLA

by Marika Ray

FOREWORD

The All-American Boy Series

Welcome to Merlot, CA, an idyllic all-American town in wine country where love is in the air, the boys are grown as fine as the wine and the town is a breeding ground for second-chances, weddings, and brand-new beginnings.

The All-American Boy Series gives you a taste of 15 of your favorite bestselling authors' brand new stories in this shared world experience. All books are standalone but may include cross-over in characters or scenes.

Grab a glass of wine, put your feet up and let us whisk you away to wine country.

The series includes the following books:

Sierra Hill *The Boy Next Door*
Poppy Parkes *Boy Toy*
Evan Grace *The Boy Scout*
Emily Robertson *The Boyfriend Hoax*
Kaylee Ryan and Lacey Black *Boy Trouble*
Kimberly Readnour *Celebrity Playboy*
Marika Ray *Backroom Boy*
Leslie McAdam *Boy on a Train*
KL Humphreys *Bad Boy*
Nicole Richard *Hometown Boy*
Remy Blake *That Boy*
Stephanie Browning *The Boy She Left Behind*
Stephanie Kay *About a Boy*
Renee Harless *Lover Boy*
SL Sterling *Saviour Boy*

INTRODUCTION

Getting mixed up with the boss's daughter was never advised, but this winery heiress has a rebellious streak that makes me want to break all the rules.

Lukas

With dreams of owning my own winery, I moved to Merlot, California for the summer to learn about the winemaking business from a local winery. I would need to seize this opportunity if I stood a chance of succeeding on my own. Then the owner's beautiful daughter came home from college. Her job? To work alongside me. Suddenly I have problems remembering my priorities.

Delta

As the heir to Black Bishop Winery, I was expected to take over soon, which was why Daddy forced me to work all summer, learning the ins and out of the winery. What he didn't count on was me learning the ins and outs of a small town boy named Lukas—someone Daddy would never approve of.

Introduction

When our young love gets tested, I'm left wondering if we can overcome the challenges our different worlds present...or were my parents right after all?

1

 Chapter 1

$\mathcal{L}$ukas

"Thank you, sir. I appreciate you taking a chance on me."

I shook the man's hand, a trickle of doubt creeping in at how soft his palm felt against mine. Growing up just barely clinging to the middle-class lifestyle in a small town, I put a lot of stock into a man having some callouses on his hands to show me his character. But Mr. Bishop was giving me an opportunity I couldn't pass up: the chance to work the back room of a winery in Sonoma Valley, learning the ins and outs of a successful business.

This was step one of achieving my dream, and a lack of callouses wasn't going to stop me.

"You bet, Lukas. Here's the key to the pool house and I'll see you tomorrow at eight sharp." Mr. Bishop placed a shiny gold key in my hand and sat back down behind his fancy desk, already moving on to his next task.

I hustled out of the room, and nodded goodbye to the various employees milling around the impressive winery that had been featured in architecture magazines over the years for its modern lines of glass and concrete. Starting tomorrow, I'd probably be getting to know those same people while I learned my position behind the scenes. At twenty, I was old enough to work the tasting room, but that wasn't how things worked apparently. You started at the bottom rung and worked your way up. Good thing I had absolutely zero problem with that. In fact, I wanted to learn every single thing that went on with running a successful winery.

So I could copy it and open my own one day.

Wild dreams for a poor kid from a small town, but I had the American dream buried in my heart, pumping through my veins, and filling me with the motivation to prove it could be done. Some might say being hired to wash dishes for almost minimum wage and living in a rich man's pool house wasn't exactly living the dream, but I could see beyond all that to ten years down the road.

Hopping on my motorcycle, I surveyed the vineyards as far as the eye could see before strapping on my helmet and heading over to Mr. Bishop's house. I'd applied for the job online, but my brother-in-law had put in a good word for me, having been a successful businessman for years up and down California. I secretly hated that I hadn't gotten the job on my merit alone, but I was too desperate to begrudge the help. The summer loomed ahead of me and I was ready to put the work in to realize my dream.

"Well, holy shit," I muttered to myself, making a left just down the road at the two cement pillars Mr. Bishop told me to look for. I pulled into a long driveway lined with tall green shrubs. "It's like the West Coast's version of a plantation."

A castle of a house loomed ahead, the rock façade almost hidden by bushes and trees and all sorts of shit flowering in the warm summer sun. I slowed to take it all in, wondering who the hell cleaned all those windows. I couldn't see Mr. Bishop putting in the elbow grease. A smaller path to the right of the property looked like the one Mr. Bishop had described. I cringed at the engine noise that bounced off the stone house, interrupting the serene gardens that flanked the acre lot. There, behind and to the side of the infinity-edge pool, sat a miniature version of the front house, vines growing up the front and everything. That would be my new home away from home for the summer and I was damn grateful.

I cut the engine and put the kickstand down, climbing off the bike I'd worked on almost every day the last year until it looked brand new. The small duffel bag strapped to the back was a pitiful display of how little I truly owned. I just didn't care about clothes. Not when that money could be saved up for the plot of land I had in mind on the far southern outskirts of Auburn Hill, the town I grew up in, just a two-hour drive south. I threw the bag over my shoulder and pulled my new house key out of my jeans pocket.

Damn, the pool looked like an oasis I wanted to explore with its blue tile and gently rippling surface of cool water, but I didn't think that part of the property was available to a lowly employee like me. Instead, I headed into the pool house and surveyed my new home.

The air inside was stale, reminding me of the old church Dad would open up every morning. Growing up a pastor's kid hadn't been easy, but helping my dad in the summers had been one of the highlights. Throwing my bag down on the hardwood floor, I went through the kitchenette and opened the sliding window, then into the single bedroom and did the same. A chrome ceiling fan in the middle of the main room off the kitchenette was a nice find. Once that sucker got cranking, the whole place aired out just fine.

I spent the rest of the day putting clothes and toiletries away, hopping back on my bike to visit the closest grocery store for supplies, and reading up everything I could find about Black

Bishop Winery. I may only be washing dishes, but I'd know that winery backward and forward from day one.

An owl hooted outside the kitchen window, pulling me out of a riveting description of the red varietals Black Bishop Winery had started with back in 1920. I blinked and realized it had gotten dark out. A quick glance at my watch showed it to be well past my usual dinnertime. I put down my research and headed for the kitchen to slap together a turkey sandwich. That was the extent of my cooking knowledge and what I'd lived on since Mom quit making my lunch sometime in high school. She'd hoped my lack of a good meal would spur me on to learn how to cook some basic dishes. She'd been sorely disappointed.

After gulping down my sandwich and a soda, I stretched my hands above my head and decided to get outside for some fresh air now that the temperature had cooled down. I grabbed the black leather jacket I wore when riding my bike and headed out. All the lights were on in the main house, lighting it up like a realtor would be coming by to take glossy pictures of what several million dollars could get you in Sonoma Valley.

The vineyards lay south of the house, so I headed in that direction. If I walked long enough, I knew I'd hit the main drag of Sonoma where the tasting rooms got closer together and the restaurants and shops sprouted up. Not being the most social guy, I had no plans on walking that far and seeing actual people. It was just me and the budding grapes on row after row of gnarled grapevines. By late summer or early fall, the grapes would be harvested, but for now, the vigneron would be watching the growth carefully. The wind swept through the plants, perfuming the air with a scent of sweetness and earth. I inhaled deeply, caught up in the differences between Sonoma and home, loving every minute of my alone time.

A flickering light up ahead caught my attention, but it was the giggle that had my ears perking up. Around the slight bend of the vineyard, a young woman came staggering up the dirt path, nearly wiping out multiple times in her platform shoes.

I sneered at the sight. What the hell was she doing walking on a dirt path in the dark in heels? As she approached, her nose stuck to the screen of her cell phone, she wasn't even looking around for strange men who might pounce at the sight of her short skirt and oblivious nature. I kept walking, her lack of concern for her own safety none of my business.

We were only ten paces apart when she startled and looked up, blinking as her eyes adjusted to the darkness around us. A strand of her long blonde hair fell across her face, covering what looked to be pretty features. Which only made me more angry. Merlot wasn't exactly a big town with a high crime rate, but a pretty girl walking home alone in the dark seemed like asking for trouble. I had a sister who I'd lecture for days if she pulled that kind of stunt.

"Oh!" she gasped, bobbling her phone and coming to a screeching halt.

Her bubblegum pink dress, far too skimpy for a late night walk even in early summer, twirled around long, tan legs. She tilted her head to the side, a flash of earrings sparkling in the moonlight.

"Do you need help?" I asked, staying where I was so as not to startle her further.

Her mouth changed from a cute little circle to a grin so wide it showed off identical dimples on either side of her face. "No, I'm good, handsome. Just heading home." Her confident reply was ruined by a hiccup.

I frowned, trying to study her eyes in the dark. "Have you been drinking?"

The girl scoffed and waved her hand through the air like she was batting away a fly, but she listed to the side a bit. "Okay, Dad. It's just me and the grapevines out here. Perfectly safe."

She *had* been drinking. That much was obvious. As obvious

as the fact that I'd have to walk her home if for nothing else than to prevent any guilt if she showed up in tomorrow's newspaper as a dead body. Definitely not because she was the hottest girl I'd ever seen, but because it was the right thing to do. Didn't appreciate the dad reference though.

"Just you and the grapevines and yet I found you. How about I walk you home, princess? Make sure you get there safely." I still didn't come closer though she showed no signs of being scared of me.

She shrugged and even that looked cute on her. "Suit yourself." She gave me the once-over and I could feel her gaze linger across my chest. "You don't happen to have a spare pair of shoes under that jacket, do you?"

The question was so absurd I couldn't hold back the bark of laugher. "No, definitely not." I came to my senses and shrugged out of the leather jacket, finally approaching her. "But here, why don't you wear that so you don't get cold."

It may have been the moonlight playing tricks on me, but I could have sworn she blushed. She let me get close enough to drape it across her shoulders, the scent of something sweet and fruity drifting up to my nose. I leaned in closer when I should have backed away.

"Wow, a real live fucking gentleman, huh? Daddy would love you. Too bad all he got was a worthless daughter."

Her words hit me and I jolted back, giving her space while we started to walk. I kept my pace slow in deference to her ridiculous choice of footwear. The girl was sweet to the eyes and nose, but she had a mouth on her. Color me intrigued.

"Nothing gentlemanly to want to make sure a girl gets home safe. I don't want to be a suspect in a murder case having been the last one to see you alive."

She chuckled and then tripped on a rock. I grabbed her elbow and pulled her back up, her soft skin registering even as I wanted to roll my eyes at her. She adjusted my jacket on her shoulders and kept going.

"I don't know about that..." She paused and then squinted up at me. "I don't know your name."

I looked straight ahead, guessing we had another half a mile to the Bishops' house. Who knew how long we had to walk to this girl's place?

"It's Lukas. You?"

"Delta. Not princess."

I smirked. Ah, she had a sense of humor. "And how far are we walking tonight?"

She pointed ahead, her arm ramrod straight. "To the castle!"

"Um, and for people new in town, where would that be?"

She dropped her arm and wrapped it around mine, snuggling in close. I certainly didn't mind, though taking advantage of a girl who'd been drinking was on my list of things never to do. I'd had right and wrong engrained in my head for too many years to cross that line.

"The Bishop estate. The one with all the stone."

Warning bells clanged in my head, and suddenly I didn't want her wrapped around me like that, as nice as it felt.

"Are you Mr. Bishop's daughter?" I asked quietly, glad there was no one around to hear this conversation or report back to my new boss that I was walking around in the dark with his only daughter. My research into his winery had revealed that while the winery had been passed down to the Bishop sons for several generations, there was only one daughter in the current generation, raising speculation on if she'd eventually sell it all or take over the business herself.

"Yep! The one and only daughter to the great Black Bishop Winery empire."

I sensed dark sarcasm and a whole truckload of daddy issues. I was also highly aware of each part of her soft body that pressed against mine as we walked. That fruity scent—was it mango?—

floated all around me, driving me crazy. Why did girls have to smell so good?

We came up on top of a hill, the lights on in the Bishop house illuminating the rest of our walk. I couldn't think of a single thing to say back to her. Part of me wanted to stop time and turn her toward me. Maybe take her face in my hands and memorize everything about her right before I kissed her. Find out if she tasted as sweet as she smelled.

The other part of me wanted to run away as fast as I could. I wasn't here to get messed up with a girl. Especially not this girl. I was here to learn everything I could so I could eventually open my own place. Be my own boss. Start my own empire.

A kiss with a drunk girl under the moonlight wasn't worth tossing away this opportunity.

I came to a halt beneath an old oak tree, the branches blocking out some of the light streaming out of the Bishop house. Tugging gently, I pulled my arm away from her and stepped back. My hands went into my pockets where they wouldn't make the mistake of reaching out and touching that soft skin.

"This is the end of the line for me. I can watch from here to make sure you get in okay."

Delta tilted her head again, her eyes unfocused. "Okay, handsome."

She lifted up on her toes, her hand bracing herself on my chest. Her lips puckered and my whole body froze. Shit. She was going to kiss me.

I turned my head at the last second, her kiss glancing off my cheek before she rocked back on her heels, unsteady as usual on her feet. She frowned at me and then winked, a combination that probably made sense in her alcohol-fuzzy brain.

She spun and walked off down the path. I watched her go, my gaze unable to focus on anything but the way the ends of her blonde hair swung right above her gorgeous ass with each step. I scrubbed a hand over my face and glanced around, making sure no one saw me. Halfway home, she turned back around, my leather jacket still on her shoulders.

"Too bad you're a gentleman, handsome!"

She grinned and turned back around. I nearly swallowed my tongue, knowing exactly what had been on the table had I wanted to go there. My dick was pissed at my morals, unable to find enough room in my jeans after walking with Delta Bishop. As soon as she was in the back door of the house, I rushed down the path, veering left and heading straight to the pool house, slipping inside and locking the door.

"Fuck!" I said to my empty room.

I flopped down on my bed and grabbed my cell phone to text my buddy Dante that I'd arrived in Merlot in one piece, which I'd forgotten to do when I first got here. He hadn't been happy when I got the job and decided to leave Auburn Hill for the summer. But he knew how much my dream meant to me and promised to support me. That was what best friends did.

After that was done, I stripped off my jeans and T-shirt and climbed into bed. I could have sworn I still smelled that mango scent. As soon as I laid my head down on the pillow, my hand shoved into my boxers and wrapped around my dick. It was still semi-hard from the encounter with Delta. Just thinking of her thick lips and sweet dimples had me hard and ready. I stroked up and down twice, rubbing hard enough to cause pain. I didn't want to be beating off to the vision of Delta Bishop, but that's exactly where my brain went. Envisioning those lips around my cock had me breathing hard. A few more tugs and the thought of her hair all around me, I'd made a mess on my stomach.

"Fuck," I whispered, getting up again to clean up.

That shit couldn't happen again. "Just put her out of your head and focus, Lukas," I pep-talked myself.

I was here to learn.

Period.

9

2

lta

"Delta!" Daddy's tone was far too harsh for the headache brewing between my eyes that morning.

I took another sip of coffee before turning around and answering him. "Yes, Daddy?"

"Did you read through the folder I gave you last week? I need you ready." He grabbed the plate of eggs and toast Mom handed him, smoothing his tie and sparing me a quick glance.

My stomach churned, a result of too much alcohol and not enough food in the last twenty-four hours. I couldn't really blame myself though. It had been my last day of freedom before a summer of enslavement by my own father. No matter how many times I told him I wasn't sure if running the winery was what I wanted to do with my life, he insisted on involving me anyway. The school year had just ended and here I was in a pair of black slacks and a starched white shirt bright and early on Monday morning, reporting for duty.

"Yes, Daddy. I read through it all like you asked."

I would never share the fact that I'd been insanely interested to see the profit margin of an established winery. The number of zeroes had surprised me, even though we'd never been hurting for money and I lived in one of the most expensive houses in Merlot. Assuming and knowing were two different things.

We were filthy fucking rich.

"We only have the summer before you go back to Stanford, so you'll be doing double duty. You'll work the lowest jobs just like I did and just like my dad and granddad. I'll also be pulling you into some higher-level meetings, so clear your calendar for the next two months."

He exited the kitchen with Mom to eat breakfast at the long dining table. That was that, I guessed.

"Yes, Daddy," I sighed to the empty kitchen. I grabbed a piece of toast and jammed it in my mouth, knowing I'd need the calories to get through working whatever menial jobs he threw my way.

Glancing down at my cherry pink nails, I sighed again, thinking about all the salon trips with my sorority sisters and the wild parties and the late nights giggling in our dorm room. Being home under my parents' watch was going to be like a punch to the dick. Unwelcome and painful.

"This is Rosie. She's the manager for the tasting room. Once you graduate from the back room, you'll report to her." Daddy swept through a doorway after pointing out a tall brunette behind the long countertop.

She smiled at me and I waved back before rushing after Daddy. He'd already introduced me to five other people as we went through the winery and I'd promptly forgotten all their names. Didn't people believe in name tags anymore?

"Sure Rosie doesn't need an extra hand pouring today? I read up about every varietal." I floated it out there, full of both hope and desperation. If I had to work at the winery all summer, it would be really great to be out there where I could chat up the customers and keep things interesting.

Daddy tossed a dark look over his shoulder. "Nice try."

I sighed and resigned myself to my fate.

The wooden floors were just as nice in this new area, but the lighting was terrible and the furnishings were sparse in the huge room I found myself in. A single person stood bent over an industrial steel sink against the far-left wall, up to his elbows in soap suds. A smattering of steel appliances surrounded him. Ah. We must have arrived at the infamous back room. The place I'd earn my street cred before being allowed to play with the big kids in the tasting room.

Daddy spread his arms out and grinned. "This will be your domain. No detail is too small, no effort goes unnoticed. Do your best work here and I'll know you're ready for more. Today you'll work on cleaning all the glasses from the weekend rush, restock the wines out front behind the bar, and inventory the cheese and crackers so we know what needs ordering. Aprons are over there."

He gestured to a small coat closet of sorts before giving me a pat on the back and walking out, whistling. I put my purse away, sliding my phone into my pants pocket, and grabbed a black apron emblazoned with our company logo. I always thought the two gold B's wending around a bishop-shaped chess piece looked a bit like they were wrapping around something more phallic, but I never shared that with Daddy. I couldn't help a chuckle as I tied the apron around my waist. That would not have gone over well.

I spun around and took in the room. The guy at the sink hadn't even turned around, so I figured I'd leave him to the glasses and find my own project. The wall of floor-to-ceiling built-in wine racks seemed interesting, so I walked over there and found a clipboard. Inventory. I could do that.

An hour later and I decided that I'd sat through biochemistry lectures that were more riveting than taking inventory. A throat clearing behind me made me jump and nearly drop the clipboard.

I turned around and...well...paused.

My brain froze and my eyes widened like maybe then I could understand what was in front of me. Or should I say who.

The hot stranger from last night. The one whose leather jacket still hung in my room.

"L-Lukas?" I stuttered.

He looked at the ground and then back up at me, looking like he wanted to be anywhere but there. His scruffy brown hair was disheveled, like he'd swiped a soapy hand through it more than once already this morning. He made disheveled look hot with the ropey muscles straining his plain black T-shirt and dark jeans.

"Princess," he said in that deep grovel of a voice that had intrigued me last night even if he'd scared me when I first saw him in the vineyard.

But holy shit. I hadn't seen those vibrant blue eyes in the dark last night. They were practically shining at me, making me think of emeralds or sparkling Caribbean waters. I shouldn't even be noticing because I didn't care for the princess nickname. It wasn't so much the name, but the volume of innuendo behind it. He thought of me as the spoiled rich girl and that irked me. Maybe because it hit too close to home. Growing up with money meant you were always trying to outrun that quick judgement.

"Oh good, you two have met." A voice interrupted our moment, but not the staredown of each other.

A vaguely familiar mid-forties man came up to both of us, his black polo emblazoned with the company logo in gold thread. He clapped his hands together, pulling me out of my trance.

"Lukas, this is Delta. Delta, Lukas. You two will be working together this summer, so hopefully you'll get along. If you'll come this way, I will give you the official tour and then I'll give you tasks to get done this week. I'm John, by the way, the winemaking director for Black Bishop Winery."

Lukas, the ass-kisser, reached out his hand for a shake and seemed genuinely pleased to meet John. I, on the other hand, just hoped our tour lasted awhile so I could take a break from inventory. I'd heard Daddy talk about John, so I felt like I knew him already. He was married with two kids. Been working for Daddy for close to twenty years now.

John had the unique ability to walk forward, while spinning his upper body halfway around to keep talking to people trailing behind him.

"I'll be overseeing you both for two weeks while we teach you everything that goes into winemaking. After that, you'll be with the operations manager, and then after that, the vineyard manager. Seeing all sides of this business is imperative to running a successful winery. From there, Delta, you'll be placed wherever your father sees fit. Lukas, we'll have to see what side fits you most."

John kept walking down a long line of oak wine barrels while Lukas shot me a glare. I looked up at him and shrugged. Not my fault my daddy owned this winery and would give me a job. You'd think I'd start in the tasting room, not back here in the dungeon. A spoiled princess I was not.

I could feel him next to me the entire tour, his arm brushing mine on occasion, the rough hair there an intriguing sensation. The last few guys I'd dated were total gym whores, shaving their entire bodies in fear others wouldn't be able to see their muscles under the hair. Lukas didn't look like he worked out in a gym. More like he did things with his hands that led to muscles as an afterthought.

"Okay, so now you've seen the whole backroom operation."

John clapped his hands and I had to pull my head back into

the conversation. I must have missed the last few minutes while I was lost in my thoughts about Lukas. Hopefully I didn't miss anything important.

"It's impressive, for sure," Lukas said, his expression serious.

What was his deal? This was a minimum-wage job doing the crap no one else wanted to do. Was he really going to play that game where he kissed ass the whole time we worked together? Because that was going to get old. Real fast.

"Black Bishop has a long history of never cutting corners and always putting the grapes first." John's chest puffed up like he single-handedly planted the damn grapevines himself. "Now how about I get you two back to inventory and then restocking the supply in the tasting room."

John led us back to the wall of wine racks and that damn clipboard. He explained how to do what I'd already been doing and then left Lukas and me alone. The sounds of the tasting room drifted into the back, making me realize lunch crowd was starting to pick up. I grabbed the clipboard as Lukas drifted his hand over the racks, staring at the bottles of wine like he was studying for a test later.

"How about you call out which wine and how many and I'll mark it down?" My voice came out louder than I wanted, the words practically a gunshot in the silent room. I cleared my throat and tried a softer tone. "Maybe we can get done before lunch."

Lukas's laser gaze stayed on me for a beat longer than was necessary, making me shift in my black Converse high-tops. What was with this guy and his straight-faced stare that had my stomach churning?

He nodded once and gave me his back, touching each bottle of wine while he counted meticulously. His blunt-tipped fingers practically caressed each bottle neck. Butterflies hit my churning stomach and I realized that maybe I'd taken the wrong end of this job. I'd have to sit here watching him for another hour before we were done.

My head listed to the side and I allowed myself to sweep his entire body with my gaze, unhurried thanks to his focus on the wine bottles. He wore plain black Chucks that had seen better days. His jeans were already a faded black, molding to his ass quite nicely in a way you didn't see much in guys these days. Even the guys who wore tight jeans tended to sag them so badly you couldn't accurately see what kind of ass you were dealing with. But Lukas? Oh, he had a very fine ass.

"Princess?"

His voice pulled me from my thoughts. And pulled my gaze from his backside to see him looking over his shoulder at me, a smirk on his handsome face that meant he'd caught me staring at him.

My cheeks heated and I hated that he had me flustered. "Huh?"

"I said the 2015 pinot noir only has three bottles."

I quickly looked down at the clipboard like my life depended on it and wrote down the number in the appropriate column. "Got it."

Lukas went back to counting.

"And don't call me princess," I said in my best bitch voice.

Lukas only made a sound in the back of his throat that sounded an awful lot like he was laughing at me inside. The rest of inventory, we kept quiet, only calling off numbers when necessary. And I kept my eyes firmly on the clipboard.

"Ready for lunch?" Daddy broke the silence a while later, his shirt sleeves rolled up and looking at me expectantly.

I looked back at Lukas, his jaw clenched tight.

"I'll finish up here. You go ahead." He took the clipboard from me and kept going, dismissing me without a glance.

I rolled my eyes and followed Daddy out, wondering what inspirational advice he'd force down my throat while we ate lunch in his office. As much as Lukas acted pissed off that I had the attention of the owner of the winery, he didn't realize I envied him and the lack of responsibility to live up to someone else's expectations for you.

I'm not saying growing up with money didn't have its perks.

But it also came with a lot of responsibility and pressure.

3

Chapter 3

*L*ukas

After another round of cleaning glasses, where Delta immediately jumped at the less messy part of the job and left me to do the dirtiest work, we were finally done for the day. I'd learned so much my head was spinning. Didn't help that the pretty girl from last night was like my goddamn shadow. Everywhere I went I could smell her mangoes like she'd bathed in them before coming to work. She was stealing my focus and I couldn't have that.

I hung up my apron and grabbed my helmet and keys from the cabinet in the back room. More studying awaited me when I got back to the pool house. I was also thinking of walking through the grapevines and seeing if I could identify which grapes were which based on their early growth stage.

The door swung shut behind me and I sucked in my first breath of non-mango-scented air since this morning. What were the odds I'd get paired up with the owner's daughter when I was just trying to learn as much as I could this summer? I didn't move away from home and all my friends to get sidetracked by a spoiled rich girl who didn't take the winemaking process seriously.

"Hey, Lukas, wait up!"

Shit. I took a deep breath and willed my eyeballs not to roll back in my head. I paused by my bike and looked at her hustling across the parking lot to reach me, her blonde hair tumbling out of the messy bun she'd put it in when we did the dishes.

When she reached me, her cheeks were flushed and she was breathing heavy enough to make my gaze want to look at her breasts, but I was stronger than that. Maybe.

"You want to go swimming or something? We can go back to my pool." The words were rushed, almost like it was a pity invite. And I didn't do pity.

"Nah. I got things to do. See you tomorrow." I strapped on my helmet, got on my bike, and fired it up, drowning out what she said next.

Probably a dick move, but after eight hours around her, I needed some space. I needed to focus on learning about the winery, not the way she swiped her right wrist across her forehead when she got the tiniest bit sweaty. Or the way she bit her bottom lip constantly, driving me absolutely crazy.

The wind hit my arms as I rode, cooling me off and prompting me to keep going on the winding road, just to sightsee for a bit before returning to the pool house. A white Range Rover came up behind me, and after a double take in my mirrors, I realized it was Delta.

"What the fuck?" I muttered.

The turnoff for her house came up on my left, but she didn't turn, instead following me all the way into the little town of Merlot and around the wineglass-shaped fountain in the square. This time I did roll my eyes.

"Alright then. I guess you'll follow me right home and learn we're neighbors."

I sped up after the last stop sign in town and headed back toward her house, making the right down her long driveway and splitting off to the right again to go around to the pool house.

I'd barely gotten my helmet off and the kickstand down when she ran down the driveway to the pool house. She had the funniest little line between her eyebrows. Still totally hot, even when confused and slightly angry.

"You following me, princess?" I asked with a smirk, knowing the nickname would rile her up further.

She pointed to the house and spoke slowly. "This is my house."

I nodded and got off the bike. "Yes, it is. Good job."

Pulling the key out of my pocket I walked to the pool house, ignoring her angry stance.

"Oh, for fuck's sake. *You're* the guy Daddy rented the pool house to?"

My back was to her, the key in the lock, but her comment hit me like a kick to the balls. The disdain in her voice made me feel like I'd snap in two, a firecracker ready to explode.

"Don't worry. I won't rob you, princess." The words poured like venom from my mouth.

I may have been from a small town. I may have been dirt poor compared to her, but I wasn't going to let her make me feel bad about who I was. I was a good guy, just looking for experience so I could make a difference in the world. If I'd wanted to harm her or rob her, I'd have pounced last night when we were all alone and she wasn't exactly at her best.

With that I entered my new apartment and shut the door. I locked it too, just to drive home my point that maybe I should be more worried about her. She was, after all, the one who'd been walking around inebriated last night. Not me.

I threw my keys down and walked to the kitchen to grab some

water. Anything to cool down the hot temper that flared when that girl looked down her pretty nose at me. When the water didn't cut it and I still felt that lava flowing through my veins, I went into my room to change into shorts and a beat-up rock concert T-shirt that had seen better days. Dante and I had gone into San Jose our junior year of high school and saw our favorite band, Blue Is the Color. We'd had so much fun we were willing to part with almost fifty bucks apiece for official concert shirts.

Stepping back out of the pool house, I looked both ways but didn't see any sign of Delta. I went around back and jumped down the short retaining wall to a clear patch of dirt beneath a huge cedar tree. I'd seen it out my bedroom window last night and wondered just how old it had to be to have grown that big. I put my portable speaker down and connected it to my phone.

When Nick Fletcher sang the first line, I started a round of burpees to get warmed up. Then push-ups, followed by lunges, pistol squats, and pull-ups from the lowest branch of the tree. I got lost in the music, lost in the lyrics and the way my muscles and lungs screamed at me. The smell of the cedar and grapes all around me was something new and exciting. I tossed my shirt off and let the sweat wash away the stress of the day. Everything felt possible again as the anger left my system. I was just finishing with some ab exercises in between sets of burpees when Delta showed up.

She ran down the same path I'd found her on last night, this time in the tiniest pair of shorts that hadn't quite crossed the line to a bikini and a sports bra with a bazillion straps. She had head-phones in, her ponytail swinging with each step. I knew the minute she saw me. Her steps faltered and kicked up a little puff of dust.

She smiled big and ran over, popping her headphones out. My blood cooled a bit, my guard going up the closer she got. She had a killer body, a huge distraction from the bullshit that came out of her mouth. It pissed me off that my own body responded to seeing hers. I'd been aware of her at all times today and it drove me nuts. I shouldn't like her. She was nothing like me, and getting mixed up with the boss's daughter was never advised.

"Hey, Lukas," she said on an exhale.

Her eyes looked blue right then against her royal blue top. Even the shimmer of sweat on her forehead only served to make her look hotter.

"Hey," I answered back lamely.

Her gaze swept down my chest and stayed there, making me acutely aware of how little I wore at the moment.

"What are you doing out here?" she asked, still looking at my chest.

My hand came up and swiped across my chest before I could stop it. She'd literally just insulted me an hour ago and now she was checking me out? This girl was hot and cold.

I hooked a thumb over my shoulder to the shirt and speaker lying on the ground. "Working out, same as you."

She nodded and then looked up at my face, her cheeks redder than when she'd first approached. "I see that. Um, did you forget shoes?"

I looked down at my bare feet, now caked with dirt. "Nah. Who needs shoes when you have feet?"

She wrinkled her nose at that. Her face then cleared so quickly I almost missed the disdain. "I met Nick one time."

"Huh?"

She tossed her ponytail over her shoulder and stood straighter. "Nick Fletcher. The lead singer of the band you're listening to. My daddy got us backstage passes for my sixteenth birthday party. Back before Nick got married."

A warmth started up in my chest even as I tried to bat it away. She knew my favorite band. Not only knew who they were but liked them.

"Yeah, my best friend, Dante, and I went to see them in San Jose about four years ago. I've loved them ever since."

She smiled at me and I couldn't help but smile back. Suddenly I wanted her to stay. The prospect of a long evening here by myself with nothing to do but study didn't seem so appealing.

"So what are you doing out here?"

Her easy smile turned sarcastic as she broke our gaze and stared out over the vineyards. "I'm bored, Lukas, so I went for a run. I'm just a bored, rich girl looking for some excitement. If that's not a cliché, I don't know what is."

I smirked, liking her even more for acknowledging how privileged she was. "You could pick up a hobby. Donate your time. Take a summer class. Read a good book."

She looked back at me and mirrored my expression with one eyebrow raised. "I have a hobby actually. I made something, but it's not quite done yet. Once I work out the kinks, I might try to sell it to the highest bidder and get out of here."

I looked out over the fields, stepping closer to her to see if she still smelled like mangoes. "Why are you in such a hurry to leave? Looks like paradise to me."

Delta stepped close and looped her arm through mine, just like last night. "Come walk with me?" she asked, barely above a whisper.

I couldn't deny the shiver that went up my spine hearing her voice in my ear like that. Just like I couldn't deny her a walk on her parents' property. I nodded and we started walking. She steered us around, pointing out rocks and sticks, which was surprisingly sweet.

"I have walked barefoot before, you know."

She glanced over at me quickly and bit back a laugh. "I know. I just don't want you to cut your feet and then expect me to carry your ass back."

I full-out grinned. Definitely better than being by myself in that pool house. And she still smelled like mangoes. We made it into the vineyard and started down a row of grapes.

Delta pointed while we walked. "The three most prevalent wine varieties in Sonoma County are chardonnay, pinot noir, and cabernet sauvignon. These here are pinot gris grapes. Daddy always grows those, mostly because they're my mom's favorite. Which is almost sacrilegious here in wine country. To love the white wines more than the reds."

Holy shit. Sorority girl knew her wines.

"And *your* favorite?" I asked, genuinely wanting to know.

She squeezed my arm and I felt like I passed some sort of test. "Viognier."

"Ah. Sounds as fancy as you are."

Her steps faltered and I rushed to explain. "Admit it. You *are* fancy. I met you last night and you were wearing heels in a vineyard."

She laughed and kept walking with me. "Okay, fine. I can be extra sometimes. But you can't judge a book by its cover, Lukas. Isn't that right?"

We both stopped walking and turned toward each other, barely an inch of space between my bare chest and her absurd outfit.

"That's exactly right," I murmured.

I'd never really understood why men took their ladies somewhere romantic when they popped the question. Like, shouldn't the question be the most important thing, not where it was asked? But standing there with Delta, seeing the sun set behind her, row after row of gnarled grapevines spanning as far as I could see, I understood. The environment added a heavy dose of romance, even when it wasn't what you were intending.

"I'm sorry for sounding like a bitch about you living in the pool house. I'm glad you're there and I'm glad we're working together." Delta's whisper floated across the light breeze.

Her gaze danced down to my mouth and I felt the pull. I wanted to taste her, to hell with her dad and this summer job in the back room of a winery. Her body fell forward and her breasts lay against my chest. We both stared at each other, neither of us making the first move.

A loud ding drifted up from somewhere in her shorts, making us both jolt back.

"Sorry," she muttered, unzipping a tiny compartment and pulling out her cell phone.

I blew out a heavy breath and scrubbed a hand through my hair. Kissing Delta the first day on the job would have been the stupidest mistake ever. I had to pull myself together and just find a way to get along with her while we worked together this summer. Friends. Yeah. We could be friends.

"Ugh. Just one of the sorority girls giving me shit for not including her on the brainstorming session for rush in the fall." Delta rolled her eyes and put her phone back in her pocket after thumbing out a quick reply.

Looked like I'd guessed correctly. "So, you're in a sorority, huh? What college?" It occurred to me that we really didn't know that much about each other.

She nodded and followed when I turned around and headed back for the tree where I left my stuff. "Yep, I go to Stanford and I'm on the sorority committee this year. You'd think I wouldn't have to have rush all planned out the first week we're off on summer vacation, but..."

Once we got back to the tree, I pulled on my shirt and picked up the speaker. A last glance out at the rolling hills of the vineyard had me feeling calm.

"Why, again, do you want to leave all this?"

Delta looked at me intensely for a few seconds, no answer in sight. Then she reached up and took off her diamond stud earrings, grabbing my hand and placing them in my palm. I looked down at my dirty hand next to her painted nails, the flash of the diamonds looking completely out of place.

"What—"

"Take them," she said, her eyes snapping.

I didn't know what game she was playing, but I wanted no part of it. I shoved the earrings back in her hand and stepped back.

"Hell no," I spat.

She stared at me for a single beat and then gifted me with a brilliant smile, closing her fist around the diamonds. "Good for you, Lukas. Once you take the money, they own you."

Delta winked at me and walked off toward the house.

I watched her go, my jaw dropped open and my eyes eating up the way I could see the curve of her ass below her shorts. Own me? What the hell had that been about? And why did I get the sense there was a hell of a lot more to Delta Bishop than the rich-sorority-girl persona I'd painted her with?

elta

"Want to go for a run and then I'll show you the project I've been working on?" I put on the turn signal and slowed for the turn into my driveway.

It was Friday night and the end of our first week of working together in the back room of the winery. Ever since that one moment in the vineyards when I swore Lukas had been about to kiss me—and I would have let him—we'd been friends. Platonic friends who got along surprisingly well.

Without my college friends to hang with, Lukas had become my buddy. He'd gone for a run with me two days ago and I'd quizzed him the whole time about the steps in the fermentation process. Who knew all the geeky knowledge I'd acquired over my lifetime as the winery owner's daughter would come in handy with a hot guy?

"Yeah, that sounds good." Lukas shifted in the white leather passenger seat of my Range Rover, looking uncomfortable.

"What? Are my seats not right? Because I paid damn good money for cushy seats."

Lukas smirked and finally relaxed. I'd learned that about him. Get him to laugh and he instantly stopped brooding in that head of his. The guy put my resting bitch face to shame.

"Meet you out back in five?" I put the car in park in front of our five-car detached garage and hopped out.

Lukas nodded and walked down the path to the pool house. His broad shoulders barely fit in that T-shirt. Someone needed to clue him in to the fact that he needed the next size up, but it wouldn't be me. I quite liked seeing that cotton stretched across his impressive muscles. The sight did something to my insides, making me both mushy as a middle schooler with her first crush and hot as a five-alarm fire at the same time.

Once he disappeared from view, I hustled inside the house and up the wide stairs to my room, already flipping through my workout outfits in my head. I'd worn my skimpiest clothes that first day when I went for my run. I saw Lukas out the window in the back, his muscles pulling and bunching while he did pull-ups from the damn tree. Found out there was nothing hotter than a man who used what was around him to get a good workout instead of flashing his membership at a posh gym and chalking his hands to grip a metal bar. I'd wanted to push him. To see if he'd notice me in the way a woman wants to be noticed. That almost-kiss told me he did.

But that wasn't what we were. We were coworkers and reluctant friends. I wouldn't see him again after this summer, and having a fling with the renter on our property wasn't something I wanted to do when I thought things through. I mean, I loved pushing Daddy's buttons any way I could, but I had bigger battles to wage this summer. Namely, getting out from under Daddy's thumb and doing what I wanted with my career and not what he expected of me based on my last name.

So I put back the tiny shorts and put on a normal pair, made for comfort while running. An old sorority T-shirt, my running shoes, and I was ready. By the time I made it out back, Lukas was already down by the cedar tree stretching. Despite my resolve that we remain friends, he looked freaking hot in his athletic shorts. His legs had muscles and I just knew he'd look like that David sculpture when naked.

"All set?" he asked, tilting his neck right and left.

I nodded, not trusting my voice. We started running and I kept glancing at him out of the corner of my eye. I could eye-fuck him all day, but that was all I'd let myself do. Nothing wrong with a little summer eye candy to keep things fun.

"So, you going to tell me about your project?" he asked after we'd run about a half mile.

He wasn't even out of breath, while I, on the other hand, was struggling to keep from gasping and panting in his presence. Ugh. Nothing sexy about being out of shape.

"Yeah, maybe when we get back to the house?"

He nodded and kept running. A little while later, over the sound of our tennis shoes plodding over the rocky dirt path, he tried again.

"I really hope your dad didn't take offense when I made that recommendation after only two days of working at the winery."

I frowned. "No, I'm sure he—"

"It's just that I really think it could help increase sales of bottles of wine," he interjected, obviously worked up about the whole thing. "If the tasting fee is twenty dollars and our lowest-priced bottle is thirty dollars, it just makes sense to offer a free tasting with the purchase of a bottle of wine. Almost no one is going to turn down that offer. I think we could really skyrocket sales in the tasting room. We spend all this money to get them in the door. We should make sure they buy wine once they're there."

We'd reached the end of the first vineyard, approximately one mile away from my house. My lungs were screaming at me. Lukas ran way faster than I normally did. My pace was basically a fast walk disguised as a jog. I was more of an exerciser because it seemed like the right thing to do, not a goal-oriented avid runner who racked up the mileage.

"Mind if we turn around?" I gasped out.

Lukas's head snapped my direction and he seemed to notice for the first time that I was struggling. If I could have masked my heavy breathing, I would have, but survival trumped looking cute.

"Oh shit, sorry. Yeah, let's walk a bit and then run the rest of the way?"

His concern was adorable. And it made my red cheeks even hotter. Once we walked a bit, I could breathe again and I addressed his concerns.

"I doubt Daddy will be mad that you had a suggestion to make him more money," I said wryly, making Lukas smirk. "And when we get back to the house, the project I'm working on will erase all those doubts in your head. Promise."

Lukas eyed me, one eyebrow quivering like he wanted to raise it but didn't want to put in the effort. Facial expressions beyond his normal RBF were rare and precious. Until I convinced him of my project's worthiness, he'd wait to give me more than a blank stare. That was just fine by me. I believed in myself enough for the both of us.

"Race you back!" I shouted when the sight of my house came into view some two hundred yards down the path. Surely I could run that distance and not die.

I ran like the cutest boy in all of Merlot wasn't right behind me checking out my ass. I ran like my life depended on it, though mostly it was just my pride hanging in the balance. Every stomp of his feet behind me spurred me on until the joy of the race fizzled in the face of a cardiovascular system not designed for sprinting. I blamed the private chef we had at the sorority who made meals to die for. I blamed my parents for their wine-guzzling genetics. I blamed my lifestyle at college that prioritized parties instead of the gym.

But when Lukas came up beside me and then pushed me on the shoulder, making me take several steps to right myself, just as he zoomed ahead and beat me, I blamed him.

I nearly fell over trying to catch my breath. Hands on knees, I gasped until my vision cleared of the black dots and my lungs didn't hate me. Then I stood up and stumbled over to Lukas, my finger pointing to his chest. His face was split with a grin so big I didn't think it possible of him.

"You lost, princess."

"You!" Fingertip drilled into his chest. "You cheated!"

He grasped my hand, his palm rough and calloused and oh so sexy. "There weren't any rules established beforehand. Therefore, no cheating. And I won." He tugged me closer to him, our labored breathing mixing together, a sheen of sweat covering both of us.

The moment hung there and I couldn't make myself step back. He blinked and then cleared his throat, letting go of my hand.

"Come on. Enough stalling. Time to show me your project." He spun and walked toward the pool house.

I flapped a hand in front of my face, willing my cheeks to cool off. "Let me go grab my laptop."

I walked into the house and grabbed my laptop out of my room, using that time to tell myself not to be attracted to Lukas. The more I said it, the more I might start believing it. Believe it, you can achieve it. Didn't I see that on some pretty social media post all the time?

Lukas had grabbed us both a bottle of cold water, sitting on one of the lounge chairs by the pool. I sat in the chair next to him and started up the program on my computer.

"Okay, so I know I'm the sorority girl and all, but I know a thing or two about computer programs. I've been tinkering with this one since my senior year in high school, but I think I finally have it down."

Lukas leaned in close and I could smell the soap and sweat on him.

"What's the program for?" he asked.

I smiled, feeling a sense of pride puff up my chest. "It's an all-in-one tracking program made specifically for a winery. All the inventory, grape yields, timelines, bottling, and accounting you could ever ask for. Once it learns a winery's numbers, it can start making projections when you change one variable. I went ahead and implemented your suggestion about waving the tasting fee with just one bottle of wine purchased and ran the numbers. I think we can stand to make ten percent more from the tasting room with just that one change based on the number of people who come through the door and a moderate guess of one out of three who wouldn't normally buy taking us up on the offer."

Lukas leaned in even closer and then used the track pad to scroll down over my data. My heart beat faster, letting someone actually see what I'd been working on for the last couple of years.

He sat back and stared at the huge cedar tree down below the pool area. When he didn't say anything, my heart dropped. Shit. Was my program that bad? I really thought it had the potential to be amazing.

"Lukas?" I asked quietly.

He looked over at me, his face unreadable but there was definitely something there in his sparkling blue eyes.

"Holy shit, Delta. This is amazing. How'd you learn to program?"

I huffed out a huge breath, a smile forming before I could even answer. "I, uh, picked up a hobby. When I got bored, I watched videos online and then started working with various people around the world on our own projects. I have friends all over who I've never met, but they helped me make my program while I helped them with theirs. It was kind of fun, to be honest."

"Kind of fun?" Lukas sat up again. "Delta, you could sell this program all up and down the coast of California. What programs do wineries currently use?"

I sat up too, really getting into it now that I knew Lukas was into it too. "That's the thing. Most wineries are using multiple programs for each department of the winery. I haven't seen a program yet that combines them all, from planting of the grapevines to the finished bottle in the customer's hands."

"Have you shown your dad?"

I lifted a shoulder and let it fall like I didn't care. "Nah. I wanted to test it a bunch before I showed it to him."

Lukas frowned. "How long have you been testing it?"

I bit my lip and debated whether to tell him the truth. Ultimately, I figured Lukas would give it to me straight. "I've been plugging our winery's numbers into it for a year now."

Lukas's eyes widened. "And? Any problems?"

I shook my head, even as I felt a little stupid. "Nope. It's been one hundred percent accurate, even when I run the prediction models."

"Delta!" Lukas came to life, scrambling out of his chair and standing over me. "You need to show your dad and see if he can start using it. If this program works that well, it should be marketed and sold. You could be sitting on the next big tech advancement in the winery business."

His enthusiasm had my own heart pounding. Maybe this wasn't some side hobby that would amount to nothing. Maybe I really did have something worthwhile on my hands. I hopped up and took my laptop with me.

"Okay. You're right. I need to at least try. Let's go talk to Daddy."

Lukas's smile faded a bit. "Why don't you talk to him. It's your program."

I frowned. "But it's your idea about waiving the tasting fee that could raise profits. We both have to talk to him."

Lukas dropped his head and then looked back up at me, his careful mask of indifference back in place. "Okay, let's go."

∿

"So, you see, lowering the tasting fee to just one sold bottle will increase profits by at least ten percent," I said while using my index finger to point out my calculations to Daddy.

Gaining an audience with him was like trying to have tea with the Pope. Nearly impossible. Daddy sat at his huge desk in his study at home, fingers steepled and resting against his pinched mouth. He hadn't said a word the whole time I told him about my project, showed him how it worked, and ran the model with the change Lukas had suggested. To say I was nervous about his reaction would be a massive understatement. I knew my father loved me, but his criticisms had been sharp and swift my whole life.

"And this program is the type of thing that could change how wineries look at their numbers and are able to make predictions based on crops, consumer preference, and any other detail that changes year to year." Lukas had stayed quiet while I laid out the program and the new suggestion, but jumped in now to sing my program's praises.

My heart warmed hearing him come to my defense. I gave him a grateful look and he winked at me. That little wink did more to buoy my spirits than all the straight A's I'd gotten in high school and college.

Daddy dropped his hands to the arm rests of his expensive leather chair. I stood up straight and held my breath.

"This looks promising, Delta. You created this program?" He pointed at the computer screen, his expression incredulous.

I tried not to be insulted by his surprise. "Yeah, Daddy. I started it a couple years ago, but I've been tracking all of Black Bishop's numbers for the last year and it's spot on."

He nodded thoughtfully, staring at the screen. "Well done,

both of you. I'll take this all under advisement." The phone on his desk rang and he went to answer it.

"Sorry, honey. I'm expecting a call from Chateau St. Sonoma about a possible merger." He pointed a finger at us both. "Don't repeat that anywhere."

He answered the phone and we were dismissed. Lukas and I walked out. I felt oddly deflated. He hadn't disliked my program, but I didn't think he gave it as much consideration as he should have. Same with Lukas's suggestion.

"Oh, honey." Mom came rushing up to us as we walked downstairs. "Your father and I had reservations at The Wine Cellar tonight, but he can't make it. Work is never done!"

She put on a bright smile, but it looked fake like most of her smiles. She loved Daddy with all her heart, living for the moments when he gave her his full attention. They were few and far between which is why the smiles looked brittle on the edges. My mother's life was one of the reasons I didn't think I wanted to run Black Bishop wineries when I got older. If it consumed my whole life and didn't allow for a strong family bond, then why bother?

"Okay," I answered her hesitantly.

"I thought maybe you could go." Mom's blue-eyed gaze finally took in Lukas. "You could take Lukas here and introduce him to our town's oldest and finest restaurant."

She beamed, pleased with her setup.

"Oh, um, I don't know if Lukas has plans," I stuttered.

Mom latched on to Lukas's arm. "Oh, you just *have* to go. Reservations are hard to get and they'd be so upset if we cancelled last minute. Our credit card is on file, so just go enjoy yourselves, okay?"

With a final smile, she was off, leaving Lukas and me to stare at each other in awkward silence. I just got set up by my own mother, and as much as I'd love to go to dinner with Lukas, I was pretty sure a fancy dinner that sounded like a date wasn't something "just friends" should do.

"I'm game if you are..." I trailed off, biting my lip.

His gaze dipped down to my mouth, making my heart sputter. "Yeah. Dinner it is."

5

Chapter 5

$\mathscr{L}$ukas

The Wine Cellar was so not my scene, but I could fake it for an hour or two just to get the chance to stare at Delta in that little navy blue dress. The hostess walked off and I put my hand on Delta's bare back to guide her through the restaurant. Well-dressed couples took up most of the tables, the low light and hushed conversation making me feel distinctly uncomfortable. I was used to sports bars and to-go food, not multiple forks in a formal place setting.

After pushing in Delta's chair, I had a seat in mine across the table, accepting the menu that contained a lot of dishes I knew about, but had never experienced. My gut wanted out of here, but I knew all of this was experience that would help me later down the line. No one made it far in life without getting out of one's comfort zone.

"My parents love this place, and while I love the food, it's a little over the top for me." Delta smiled at me, setting her menu down and leaning her elbows on the table.

I knew she was trying to make me feel better, but she didn't need to do that. "What's your favorite type of restaurant, then?"

She shrugged. "Something a little less formal. A place where you can be yourself and not worry if you laugh too loud or use the wrong damn fork. There's a place nearby my college where we go a lot. It's cute, but not formal. Good food, nice people. An easy atmosphere."

"Sounds like Forty-Diner from my hometown." I grinned just thinking of the place where the whole town went and gossip traveled faster than the servers.

"Tell me more about this hometown of yours." Delta leaned forward, a soft smile on her face.

She had on more makeup than she did when we worked at the winery. Not that she needed it. Delta was beautiful in a classic girl-next-door kind of way. And based on her mom, she'd be beautiful with a few more lines and years on her face too.

"I was born and raised in Auburn Hill and it's your typical small town. Everybody knows your business, but it means everyone cares, you know? I can't wait to start my own business there."

Delta's grin grew and I couldn't look away. "And what business are you going to open?"

I took a deep breath, feeling a little uncertain about sharing with her. But then again, she'd gone to bat for me to her father with my idea, so I felt like I could trust her.

"I want to open my own winery, actually."

Her mouth opened in a cute little circle. "Really?"

I nodded. "Yeah. I have a little plot of land, with a handshake deal with my elderly neighbor to sell me his lot right before he passes. I should have just enough land to plant a decent vineyard.

I loved chemistry back in high school, but didn't see myself doing anything with that until I stumbled on winemaking and all that goes into it. I'm kind of fascinated."

I tugged on my collar, feeling like the button-down shirt was trying to choke me. I didn't know how men wore them all day every day.

Delta reached across the table and put her hand on mine. "Lukas, that's amazing. Now I get why you're so attentive at work. I thought you were just a kiss-ass." She smirked.

I squeezed her hand and let go, needing to not be touching her. Touching her only led to wanting her more, and I knew that was definitely crossing a line.

"Thanks a lot," I said wryly, winking to let her know I wasn't actually offended. "What about you? What's your career goal?"

Delta blew out a heavy breath. "God, I don't know. I know Daddy wants to groom me to take over Black Bishop, but I have other things I want to do too. I want to do something that's all mine, you know? Like, my eventual success has nothing to do with everything being handed to me. I want to know I did it all on my own."

I nodded, even more impressed with her. I'd judged her unfairly when we first met. Every day I learned something new about her that made that judgement crumble.

"I do know what you mean. We share that desire."

We stared at each other for a beat and I knew we shared more than just a desire for a career. There were most definitely other desires we had too. Based on the way she bit her lip and her eyes went soft, I'd bet she felt the same pull that I felt. The one that said we should scratch that itch and step across that line of friendship.

"Good evening, folks. What can I get you started with this evening?" The server interrupted our stare, startling us both.

Delta gave the server her dinner and drink order smoothly,

melting into this environment with ease. My order was a bit more stiff as I doubted my pronunciation of everything, but I got it done and soon we were left alone again.

The rest of dinner went smoothly, and despite my irritation at not fitting in, the food was outstanding. Delta and I kept up the conversation, learning more about each other and sharing our food. Dante was my best friend back home, but even he and I didn't have deep conversations about dreams, parents, and how we wished we were different. But with Delta, all that stuff flowed easily.

As we left, I kept my palm on the bare skin of her back, the smooth silk feeling driving me crazy in the best way. The sun had set and the little white lights were lit up all over downtown Merlot. We walked for a bit, checking out the shops. I was having such a good time I didn't want the night to end.

Delta came to a stop right at the wineglass-shaped fountain in the town square. The water splashed as it hit the pool below it, the perfect overflowing glass. She pulled two pennies out of her tiny purse and gave one to me.

"Time to make a wish, handsome." She gave me a wink and wrapped her arm around mine, a move I was coming to associate with only her. She liked to be touching and damn if I didn't like it too.

She pinched her eyes shut and her mouth moved like she was silently making her wish. Then her eyes popped open and she tossed the penny, the plop it made reaching us as it sank to the bottom.

"Now your turn." She laid her head on my shoulder and gave me time to make my own wish, even though I didn't believe for a second that these penny wishes came true. You had to make your own dreams come true. Wishing and hoping never worked. But for Delta, I'd do it, just to see her smile.

I thought about what I wanted, dismissing the career-oriented wishes. If I was to be whimsical by making a stupid wish, I'd make the wish whimsical too. Once the wish was firm in my head, I tossed the penny and watched it sink close to Delta's.

Her head popped off my shoulder and she spun us around so she could see me. "What did you wish for?"

I faked outrage. "You're not supposed to tell people your wish or it won't come true!"

She gave me a dirty look. "Oh, please. Tell me right now. I have to know."

"Tell me yours first," I countered.

"Fine. I wished for a kiss in the moonlight with a handsome man." Her cheeks went pink but she kept her gaze on me without even a flutter of eyelashes.

Fuck. All that time spent telling myself she was just a friend and coworker wasn't working tonight. Not by a long shot. My dick decided he wanted more, and waiting to take matters into my own hand when I got home just wasn't going to cut it.

"Delta," I muttered, reaching up to push a strand of hair behind her ear that had blown into her face.

"What was your wish?" she whispered, leaning into me so far I could see exactly how close the ends of her long eyelashes were to her eyebrows.

"It wasn't that," I whispered, trying desperately to put some space between us again or to steer this conversation back into a neutral place where I couldn't crash headfirst into trouble.

"Was it about me?" She bit her lip, the one thing I couldn't seem to resist.

I nodded.

"You should totally kiss me and see if we can't make both our wishes come true," she whispered, her eyes daring me to deny her.

She was right. I should. Here she was offering herself on a silver platter and I was shutting her down. For what? A summer job that would be over before we knew it? What harm could one kiss really do?

I brought my hand back up to her face, cupping her jaw and rubbing my thumb against that bottom lip that drove me crazy. It was soft and pillowy, just like I'd imagined it. Her tongue darted out and met the tip of my finger, sending me right over the edge of sanity I barely clung to. I angled her head where I wanted her and leaned down to kiss her. Our lips barely touched, then parted for a gasp of breath, and finally collided again in a heated kiss of lips and tongues.

Delta wrapped her arms around my neck and matched my enthusiasm. Her little groans were enough to keep me coming back for more, oblivious to everyone around us or who might see us. The only thing that mattered this summer was this kiss. This moment with Delta. The exact wrong girl for me.

A shrill whistle had me breaking away, battling a cloud of confusion. That kiss might have stopped time and transported us elsewhere. I blinked several times and the fountain came back into view, the sounds of people all around us enjoying the balmy summer night.

Delta stared at me with wide eyes, huffing like we'd gone on a run right before that kiss. "We should totally do that again."

I caught the grin before it could spread across my face and send the wrong message. My brain shouted at me to shut this down right here and now.

"Delta—"

"No, don't. Don't stand there with my lip gloss on your mouth and tell me we shouldn't have done that." She lifted an eyebrow in challenge.

I scrubbed a hand across my mouth and clenched my teeth. Clearly, she drove me crazy whether I kissed her or not. And now that I knew she tasted like cotton candy and wine and hot sorority girl all rolled into one, I knew I'd have to fight that much harder to stay away from her.

Grabbing her hand, I pulled her away from the fountain and back toward the restaurant to get her car. Her heels clicked rapid fire on the pavement beside me as she tried to keep up. I slowed down so she didn't trip and fall. When we got to her car, she pulled the keys out of her purse but wouldn't unlock the doors until I met her gaze.

"Why, Lukas? Why is us kissing again, or even dating, such a bad thing?"

I stared at her, absolutely floored that she didn't see the problem in that. "Are you kidding me? Your dad is my boss. I rent his pool house because I can't afford anything better. I'm the backroom boy of a winery while you're the winery's princess waiting in the wings to take over as CEO."

Delta scoffed, pushing out those full lips that our kiss had only made puffier. "Please. I've dated all kinds of guys and my father doesn't get a say in who they are or what their income is. You're just running scared."

She waved her hand like she saw this kind of thing all the time, a little smile on her face. And it pissed me right off. I knew I was feeding into her plan and yet I couldn't stop myself.

"Delta. I can't take you on fancy dates. Hell, I didn't even have a car to take you to this date put together and paid for by your parents. You wouldn't want to date me. Trust me."

She raised her arm and ran her finger over my chest. "Try me."

"What?" She needed to stop touching me. I couldn't think.

"Ask me out on a date. An official Lukas date. And if I can't hang, then we go back to being coworkers. Let *me* decide if I want to date you or not."

I nodded slowly, knowing that agreeing with her would be the stupidest thing I could do. "Fine. One date. Next Friday. And when you decide slumming it isn't for you, I'll say I told you so."

Her eyes flashed in the light of the streetlamp. "Deal. But I seal all my deals with a kiss."

She tugged on my collar and I fell into her, our lips finding each other and knowing exactly what to do. And if my hands slid down her back and grabbed her ass, pressing her firmly into my growing erection, she'd only have herself to blame.

She'd pushed me.

And I was falling hard.

elta

"Close your eyes," Lukas shouted at me, the wind pulling at his words.

We were flying down the road on his motorcycle, my legs and arms wrapped around him from behind. I'd only been on a motorcycle once before when my uncle was showing off his brand-new Harley. This was an entirely new experience, having the guy I was crazy about between my legs while the motor created vibration below us. I could have ridden for miles and miles on the back of this thing with Lukas, but he was pulling off the road all too quickly.

"Okay!" I shouted back, squeezing my eyes shut and willing myself to go along with the surprise. I wanted so badly to see what he'd planned for us. For this date he'd put together on his own.

The week had flown by, all the menial tasks at the winery made better by having Lukas at my side. Plus all the sneaky kisses away from security cameras had made things interesting, while making me want him with an urge stronger than I'd ever felt before. I went to bed every night thinking of him and staring at his leather jacket hanging on the back of the chair in my room. If I could help it, I'd never give it back to him.

The motorcycle came to a stop and we leaned. I listened for the kickstand and felt Lukas pivot to get us both off the bike safely. Once standing, I fumbled to get the helmet off, knowing I looked ridiculous in it. It smelled brand new when Lukas handed it to me and I wondered if he'd bought it just for this date. Keeping my eyes closed was killing me. The anticipation of what he'd put together for our date had kept me guessing all week.

Lukas cleared his throat like he was nervous. "Okay, open."

I popped those eyes open faster than Christmas morning and took in a familiar field. We were on the very edge of our vineyard property, the huge oak tree in the corner lit with a million little white lights under the canopy of leaves. A red blanket lay on the ground under the tree, a basket waiting for us. I gasped.

The scene was more beautiful than any fancy restaurant.

And more precious because Lukas had obviously put in the time to make this special for me.

A bolt of something fringing on giddy ran through me and I spun toward him to wrap my arms around his neck. "It's beautiful. Thank you," I whispered.

I felt him chuckle before he pulled back, grabbing my hand and tugging me toward our date. "It's not fancy, but we are all alone, so I consider that the tradeoff."

My face felt hot and that giddiness moved south. I liked the sound of that. Alone with Lukas. He helped me down onto the blanket while he turned on a speaker and started some soft music. Then he opened the basket and pulled out a white wine that I'd told him earlier in the week was my favorite out of all the Black Bishop wines.

"Hey! How'd you get that, Mr. Not Quite Legal?"

Lukas winked at me. "I have my ways and my sources, none of which I can divulge."

I bit my lip to keep from smiling from ear to ear. This was already more fun than I'd ever had on a date. Glancing around at the vineyard behind us, I had to admit it made a romantic backdrop.

"Here you go." Lukas handed me a glass of wine and poured one for himself before settling in next to me to watch the sunset.

I tried to watch it too, but mostly I was distracted by the way his shoulder would bump mine occasionally. Or the way his throat bobbed as he swallowed. Or the scent of cologne coming off him that I hadn't smelled on him before today. Lukas was good looking in a boy-becoming-a-man way. He had a jawline that was on the cusp of sharpening into the type that made grown women swoon. Long, unruly hair that always looked unkempt in the best of ways. Bright blue eyes that made you want to stare into them and dig for his secrets. He didn't speak unnecessarily, making each time he did feel like a treasure he entrusted you with. He may only be here for the summer, but I intended to enjoy the hell out of our time together while I could.

"Delta?"

I blinked and saw that the sun had set and Lukas was looking at me expectantly.

"I'm sorry?"

He smiled and tried again. "Ready for some dinner?"

I nodded and helped him pull containers out of the basket. "I see you got takeout."

Each container looked different, leading me to believe he'd gone to multiple places.

Lukas shook his head. "You don't want to taste my cooking, trust me. So, I went and got all your favorite dishes. Or, at least, the ones I know about."

He dipped his head and got busy opening all the containers while I gaped at him. He remembered my favorites from conversations we'd had and then went to multiple restaurants for them? This boy was trampling all over my heart. If I wasn't careful, he'd burrow himself right in there whether I wanted him to or not.

"Here you go." Lukas handed me a loaded plate.

I took the plate and put it down on the blanket next to me. Without wasting time second-guessing myself, I hooked a hand behind his neck and pulled him to me for a kiss. I didn't stop until we both pulled away breathless. Keeping my forehead against his for a moment longer, I whispered, "Thank you, Lukas."

We ate, the conversation between us always a mix of playful, serious, and deeper than any conversation I'd had with someone my age. Lukas knew a lot about everything, and he always asked the most amazing questions. He seemed like a scholar of life. Someone who loved learning. Just being around him made my own brain come alive with excitement and possibility. There was so much going on behind that brooding frown of his and I was glad I'd gotten to know the real Lukas.

"Care to dance?" Lukas stood and extended his hand out to me.

Putting down my almost empty plate on the blanket, I put my hand in his. He tugged gently and I popped up. The night had gone completely dark around us, leaving us in the glow of the lights strung above us. For the first time that night, I became highly aware we were alone. Just a handsome date and the hoot of an owl not far away.

His hands landed low on my hips, the heat of him soaking through my jeans and warming me up inside. We swayed to the slow song, just staring at each other. The silence was charged, like we both had something to say, but we felt too much to get the words out. He pulled me closer and I went willingly, our bodies now pressed together as if we needed the body heat.

"You know I think you're more than just a spoiled princess,

right?" he whispered finally. "I tease you, but I see you. All of you."

I felt a connection deep in my gut. So many people in my life saw one side of me and that's it. The rich daughter. The sorority girl. The pretty girl with a quick smile. The tech geek with a passion for programming. I was all of those things, but I was also so much more. The fact that Lukas could see all of me was the sexiest thing a man had ever said to me.

My hands went up into the hair on the back of his head, threading through the strands and wanting to hold him tightly so he'd stay with me always.

"I know. I see you too, Lukas. You'll do amazing things in life, I just know it." I smiled, seeing it in my head. "You make the grapes and the wine, I'll supply the marketing and the business side of things. We'd be a force to be reckoned with."

Lukas smiled back. "I'll hold you to it."

And then his lips were on mine, and his tongue took any further words out of my mouth. His hands traveled along my backside, heating my skin everywhere they went. I shifted, needing to feel how much he wanted me. His erection pressed into my stomach and my knees nearly buckled with the want I felt.

"Delta..." he murmured, a hand now on my breast.

"Yes, please," I answered, my own hand sliding between us.

My shoulder clipped the edge of the picnic basket and Lukas grunted. My shirt hung off one shoulder, but at least the jeans were finally stripped from my legs. Lukas pushed off of me and stood, looking down at me with half-hooded eyes. He whipped his shirt off and I bit my lip. God, those muscles were hot. His hands went to the button on his jeans and I held my breath.

"Wait!" I blurted, literally the worst at timing. "Are you sure we'll be alone?"

The idea of one of the farm hands finding us and reporting back to my father would certainly put a damper on our perfect date.

Lukas's mouth lifted on one side. He slowly unzipped his jeans and my brain scrambled. "I talked to the supervisor about bringing a date out here. Don't worry, I didn't mention your name, but he assured me we'd be alone all night."

I rolled my eyes. "Pretty sure of yourself, huh?"

Lukas tugged the jeans off and stood in his boxers, a delicious bulge looking like it wanted to be freed by my hands. No, my mouth.

"Just hopeful and equally determined to make sure you don't get in trouble for being with a guy like me."

I lifted an eyebrow. "You mean a guy who put together the most thoughtful date I've ever been on?"

He knelt by my side. "You know what I mean."

I would have argued with him longer, but he unclasped the front of my bra and dipped his head to kiss the underside of my breast before finding my nipple. There wasn't a lot of talking after that. Just his lips and tongue and teeth driving me crazy. I whimpered when his head lifted and he smiled up at me.

"You're fucking beautiful, Delta Bishop."

Something bloomed in my chest and came out in the form of a smile on my face. I'd never felt more beautiful than when Lukas Murphy nudged my thighs apart for him and swept his gaze over the whole length of my body. His finger traced down my belly and into the closely cropped curls I kept between my legs. His head dipped again, this time to zero in on my clit while his finger worked its way inside me. I gasped, the sound eaten up by the silence of the night around us. Reaching down, I wound my fingers through his hair, keeping him in place in case he dared to leave me unsatisfied.

The flat of his tongue tasted me, the tip drove me wild, and his one finger became two. Pleasure hit like a tidal wave. I felt nothing but Lukas attacking with the single-minded focus he showed with all his tasks. I briefly registered that I must have pulled too hard on his hair, because his grunt mixed with my long moan as I spiraled out into the sky.

Lukas gave me time to breathe, then his hands pried my fingers out of his hair, a smirk of devilish proportions on his face. His mouth was wet, and the sight made me blush. Most guys our age didn't bother going down on a girl, wasting no time getting to the finish line for themselves. A girl had to be quick about it or she'd miss her opportunity. Lukas, on the other hand, seemed quite pleased with himself, as he had every right to be.

"Wow. I've been missing out," I said absentmindedly, watching his muscles flex as he moved.

Lukas shoved his boxers down and pulled a condom out of the picnic basket, rolling it on and settling between my legs again. His eyes were wide. "That's the first time a guy's gone down on you?"

I nodded, my hair probably a total wreck.

"Fucking idiots." Lukas shook his head. "I'd eat you out every day if you let me."

I squeezed my eyes shut, embarrassed and turned on so much I wanted to climb him like the grapevines in the field. Where had this guy come from? And how long could I keep him?

"I'll hold you to it," I answered, flickering my eyes open to see him notching himself against me.

He slid in nice and slow, taking his time and stealing my breath with each inch. He felt so fucking good I wanted to howl at the moon and scratch my nails along his back. And that was before he began to move, the drag of his thick cock in and out in a steady rhythm driving me absolutely crazy.

Lukas held himself above me on his elbows, his shoulders straining as he drove into me. His hair was a mess from my fingers. I reached around and grabbed his ass, enjoying the flex of muscle there and loving the way he grunted when I forced him to thrust even harder.

"Delta..." he said on an exhale.

He sped up, his gaze looking like a man possessed as he took in my breasts swaying with each thrust.

"Mmm, Lukas, like that." I almost couldn't believe it, but I felt like I could orgasm again if he just kept going for another few seconds.

Lukas reached down and hooked my leg over his arm, opening me up further as my hands grabbed on to his shoulders for support. Fuck, I was glad I did yoga on the regular because bending like a pretzel was so much better when Lukas's cock was inside me.

"Look at me," he grunted.

I blinked, not realizing my eyes had closed. Lukas's jaw clenched tight, his blue eyes appearing almost black as he looked down at me. I let go of his shoulders and grabbed his face, reaching up as high as I could go to kiss him. It was sloppy, more tongue and lips than finesse, but it sent me right over the edge. I pulsed around him as I bit his lip and squeezed my eyes shut again. Stars danced behind my eyelids. His body stiffened above me and I felt his groan more than heard it.

I flopped back to the blanket, my arms sliding off his shoulders. My limbs were so far gone I couldn't have held on to Lukas if my life depended on it. He must have felt the same way since his weight crushed me while we both gasped for air.

"Holy shit, Delta," he mumbled against my neck some moments later.

I stared up at the white lights dotting the canopy of the tree. I'd never look at this corner of our property the same way again.

"Holy shit is right."

7
---

ukas

"Staff meeting in five." Delta slapped my ass as she passed, her sly little look for my eyes only.

We hadn't had much alone time together since our date last weekend. I'd thought about her every single second though. The way her eyes had gone hazy with my dick filling her. The crescent nail marks that had stayed on my back for days, reminding me of the best sex I'd ever experienced. Not that I had a ton of experience in my twenty years, but I doubted anything could surpass that night in the vineyard.

The only downside to that whole night was having to drop her off at the end of her driveway so she could walk the rest of the way home. It was on my insistence, and as much as it pained me to be her dirty little secret, I knew that's the way it had to be. Her parents would not look kindly on me dating their precious daughter.

And I guessed that was what we were doing: dating.

I finished the last glass, setting it on the counter to air dry before wiping down my arms and hands. My fingers were continually pruned from washing dishes every day. Once that task was done, I headed into the tasting room that closed for the hour every Thursday mid-morning for the staff meeting before the busy weekend started. Immediately, I spotted Delta chatting up Rosie over by the long bar. She gave me a quick wink, but otherwise acted completely normal.

We'd agreed to keep the flirting locked down while at work. It was the right thing to do.

I fucking hated it.

The tasting room door swung open and two suits walked in. If I recalled correctly, they were the head guys from Chateau St. Sonoma. Heads turned and a few whispers filled the silence. Mr. Bishop started the meeting anyway, signaling that it was okay to talk in front of the competitors.

"All right, folks, we have a busy weekend planned with our private room completely booked and a full-capacity tour coming through on Saturday. Word has gotten out about us waiving the wine-tasting fee with the purchase of just one bottle of wine and it's massively increased our foot traffic. Delta, what are the exact numbers?" Mr. Bishop extended his palm to Delta, giving her the floor for the first time in a meeting.

She stepped forward, her head held high, but I could see the blush creep onto her cheeks. My chest swelled with pride. Delta was the smartest girl I knew. If her dad wanted accurate numbers, she'd be the one to have them, and I was glad he finally acknowledged her.

"In just one week, sales from non-members have increased by fourteen point four percent. To give you a frame of reference, wine sales fluctuated four to seven percent for any given promotion in the last twenty years of Black Bishop history. We have ourselves a winner." Delta smiled and stepped back.

The assembled group of employees all clapped, knowing increased profits was a good thing for everyone. Mr. Bishop smiled smugly and let the applause go for a bit before hushing everyone. I held my breath, hoping he'd credit me with a good idea.

"I know I can count on you all to be better than your best. Let's get out there and push wine sales. Once they get a taste, I know they'll be back in the fall for memberships. And you know how happy memberships make me." He chuckled and quite a few managers smiled with him. More memberships usually meant better Christmas bonuses.

The crowd of employees walked off and I hung around, a sinking feeling in my stomach. Mr. Bishop hadn't mentioned where the idea for waiving the tasting fee had come from. I didn't technically need to get credit for it, but a little "nicely done, son" would have been nice.

"Glad you could make it on short notice. Let's get the tour going before we get slammed with afternoon tasters."

Mr. Bishop clapped one of the guys in a suit on the back, steering him toward the back room. I trailed after them, only because the rest of my tasks for the day were back there too. Anger summed in my gut. And most of it was directed at myself. I should have known a big guy like Mr. Bishop wouldn't have given credit to the backroom boy. I may have been a simple high school graduate from a small town, but I wasn't an idiot.

"I can't believe the sales increase in just a week. Think that'll continue?" the guy asked Mr. Bishop, who gave him a cocky sneer.

"Of course. When I thought of it, I knew it would be a promotion we could do forever if we wanted. Sales are sales, right?"

I nearly choked on my own spit. I gave the back of Mr. Bishop's head an angry stare. The door swung shut behind me and I turned to see Delta standing there with her hands on her hips.

She must have heard her dad too. Mr. Bishop looked back at us and then got busy moving the two guys out of the back room.

When they were out of earshot, I grabbed the clipboard that held the inventory list Delta and I were supposed to go through that afternoon and threw it across the room. It hit the stainless steel sink and clattered to the floor. Oddly, I didn't feel any better.

Delta whispered, "I'm sorry, Lukas."

"Don't." I slashed my hand through the air. "Don't you dare apologize for your father."

She bit her lip and a small part of me that wasn't raging mad felt guilty for snapping at her. It wasn't her fault her dad was an idea-stealing jackass who couldn't give credit where it was due. I'd take this experience and tuck it away in the back of my brain. I wouldn't do that to my employees.

"Let's just get this inventory done so we can leave for the day and go on our run." I marched off to grab the clipboard, unable to look Delta in the eye.

I stood with my hands on my knees, trying to catch my breath. The run had done me good. Pushing us both to a higher speed had burned off all that anger I'd felt this afternoon.

"Hey." I straightened and ran my hand down Delta's arm.

She turned toward me, hesitant. I hated that I put that look on her face, or the doubt in her head. I'd been an ass all afternoon, giving her one-word answers and generally being a black cloud. I was better than that.

"I'm sorry. I should have handled things better."

Her face softened and she tugged on my sweat-soaked T-shirt. "I'm exactly the person who would understand what an asshole my dad can be. He should have given you credit, Lukas."

I shrugged, now more interested in the line of skin that showed below Delta's crop top. "Whatever. This isn't the end of the road for me. There'll be plenty of chances for me to have home runs with my own winery. I'm just grateful I got to meet you."

Delta dipped her head and smiled up at me through her lashes. "Me too." She leaned up on her toes and pressed a kiss to my lips. "Hey, I have an idea. Let me go grab my swimsuit and let's hit Nathanson Creek to cool off."

A swim with Delta sounded exactly like what I needed to let go of the day. "Let's do it."

She went into her house and waved at me to follow. I did so hesitantly, even though I'd been inside her house a few times before, but only for her to grab something, and I never saw Mr. Bishop. I stayed in the doorway of her bedroom, even when she tossed me an eye roll over her shoulder. I'd crossed a lot of lines already with Delta, but being in her bedroom under Mr. Bishop's roof just seemed like one I shouldn't cross. For my own longevity.

Delta picked through a drawer and came out with a tiny strip of red cloth held triumphantly in her hand. "Got it! Let's go grab yours."

I spun around and froze, seeing Mrs. Bishop approaching, her eyebrows drawn together. She looked past me and picked up her pace when she saw Delta.

"Honey, I need you to go shower. The Hendersons will be here for dinner in about an hour."

Delta frowned. "No, sorry, Mom. I have plans."

"Well, cancel them," her mom snapped. "Your father has big plans for this merger and they need to see the next generation of Black Bishop wineries is waiting in the wings. Tradition is huge for them and us."

One look at Delta's face and I knew I shouldn't be there. World War III was about to break loose and I wasn't sure if my presence would escalate things.

"I'm not interested in being in a dog and pony show, Mother."

Mrs. Bishop stepped closer to Delta and lowered her voice,

though I could hear every word clearly. "You will be at dinner or you can kiss the funding for your next semester goodbye. And trust me when I say Stanford isn't cheap, my dear."

Delta's eyes took on a sheen. "Fine." She spun and stomped back in her room to slam the door.

The silence in the hallway was incredibly awkward. I took one step back and Mrs. Bishop spun on me, finally acknowledging my presence.

"I'm sorry you had to see that. You're a nice kid, Lukas, but we have grand plans for that daughter of ours." She lifted an eyebrow, so like Delta I could blink and see what Delta would look like in twenty years.

Her meaning was clear. Especially with her nose in the air as she swept down the hall and down the stairs. I wasn't good enough for Delta, so don't get attached.

I held myself back from punching the wall and found my way outside.

Back in the pool house I kicked the bed and decided today was the absolute shittiest of days. I made myself a sandwich and hit the shower before lying down in bed. Might as well get used to being alone. After this summer I'd have to say goodbye to Delta anyway.

My phone dinged and I saw the text was from Delta, but I couldn't bring myself to open it. Maybe it was for the best that we cool things off. The pain in my chest at the idea told me I'd already gotten in too deep. As far as I knew, she just saw me as a passing distraction over the summer. A summer fling to carry her through to when her sorority lifestyle started again.

I just needed to go back to my original motto for the summer: head down, focus on learning everything I could about wine.

"Lukas."

The whisper came from my dream, but the hand stroking down my arm felt so real I startled awake. Blinking my eyes against the dark, I saw Delta standing next to my bed, biting her lip. The watermelon sundress looked gorgeous on her, highlighting her curves and long blonde hair.

"Delta?" My voice came out gruff, still half asleep.

She reached around her back and unzipped the dress, letting it fall to the floor. I sat straight up in bed and gaped at her. She stood perfectly naked, right down to her watermelon toenail polish. Lust surged so swiftly, I tossed the covers back and pulled her down on me without even thinking. As soon as her bare skin touched mine, I knew I couldn't kick her out. Couldn't retreat to just being coworkers. She made my heart soft and my dick hard just looking into her brown eyes.

She straddled me and crushed her mouth to mine. My hips surged up against her of their own accord, seeking her heat like it was the most natural thing in the world. With her mouth still fused to mine and our tongues tangled together, she lifted up and sank down onto the first inch of me. Fuck, it felt so good I punched the mattress and waged a mental battle for a few seconds longer than I should have.

Common sense won and I pushed her back, grabbing her hips and lifting her off me. My cock hit my stomach with a thump in the silent room, a reminder he was unprotected.

"Delta," I mumbled, shocked she'd done that.

She whimpered like a whiny child, so I slapped her ass, making her yelp. "Get a condom. Hurry up!" she chided me.

I chuckled as I reached for one in the bedside table, putting it on barely a second before Delta was back to hovering and lowering herself onto me.

"Lukas, I need you," she moaned in my ear, her hair in my face and her pussy accommodating my cock ever so slowly as she sank down.

As soon as she hit the base, she lifted back up, in a hurry and knowing exactly what she wanted. I gritted my teeth and tried to slow her down with my hands on her hips. She sat up quickly and palmed her own breasts, making my mouth bone dry at the sight. She was fucking beautiful riding my cock, and I couldn't make her slow down. Didn't want that actually. Not when she had my balls drawn up so tight I was in pain. Not when she looked so close to falling over that edge like some Amazonian warrior princess intent on her goal.

She tossed her head back and I felt the flutter. That squeezing all around my dick triggered me and I couldn't stop the inevitable even if Mr. Bishop walked through that door right then and there. I barked out a groan and clenched my teeth. My eyes squeezed shut, uncertain if I'd just died and gone to heaven or if this was the absolute best dream I'd ever had.

Delta flopped back down on my chest, her hair getting stuck in my mouth, but I didn't even care. All that mattered was her thundering heart right on top of mine.

"Promise me we'll do this thing together," she gasped out, her lips smashed against my chest.

I couldn't think straight. "Do what?"

"Two years from now, when I'm done with school and you've learned everything there is to learn about winemaking, we'll go out on our own. You and me."

She sat up again, her hair a mess and her cheeks still flushed, but her eyes looked more direct than I'd ever seen them. If my heart had thundered before, now it galloped at the idea of Delta wanting something long term with me.

"You and me?" I asked, just to clarify that she really meant it.

She bit her lip and nodded.

"Fuck, yes," I answered, meaning every word.

Then I flipped her over and kissed her like we had our whole life planned out.

Together.

8

Chapter 8

elta

The next two weeks passed in a roller coaster of work, events my father strong-armed me into attending, and stolen moments with Lukas that set my soul on fire. He and I were becoming a team. A rock-solid team despite us just being two kids with lofty dreams. I knew there'd be challenges we'd face, but I also believed we could face them together and come out the other side an even stronger pairing.

I had exactly thirty days until I had to head back to Stanford and prepare for a new group of girls to rush before the fall semester. Thirty days to get my fill of Lukas. Which was hard considering we'd decided to keep our relationship a secret from everyone for the time being. Like it or not, I depended on my parents' open wallet to get my degree at college. I knew a relationship with Lukas would be like waving a red flag in front of a bull. My parents would yank my college funding without blinking an eye. And I needed that degree to set us up for a successful winery together.

"What the hell are you wearing?" A girl's snappy voice brought my attention back to the here and now as I stepped out of my car.

I looked up and saw five overly dressed girls with expensive handbags, perfectly curled hair, and varying expressions of welcome and disbelief standing in my parents' driveway.

"My girls!" I yelled, running over and hugging them as they surrounded me.

They giggled and whooped, their energy over the top with excitement, just like old times. My friends. My sorority girls who I did everything with at school, were here in Merlot.

"What's going on?" I asked as the hugging finally stopped.

"More importantly, what's up with that outfit?" Natalie asked, looking like she bit into a lemon.

I rolled my eyes. "It's a work outfit. You know? For an actual job?"

I didn't blame her. I hadn't worked a day outside of helping my parents with the winery. I wouldn't have known about white collared shirts and black slacks until this summer either.

"So, you're actually working working?" Blair chimed in.

"Yes—"

The thrum of a motorcycle engine cut off whatever I was going to say to make them understand that I was holding down a big-girl job with a paycheck and everything. All six of our heads turned to the driveway to see Lukas coming home from work. His sunglasses reflected the trees overhead and his forearms flexed as he steered to the right. He nodded once and I had to bite my lip from smiling like a lovesick fool. My boyfriend was hot on any given day, but even hotter on his motorcycle.

"Who. Is. That?" Bree asked, her jaw dropped.

I broke my gaze away from Lukas's retreating back. "That's

Lukas. He rents the pool house and works at the winery with me."

Natalie squealed. "Why didn't you tell us about him? He's hot!"

"I wouldn't mind going for a dip in the pool right now." Anna started walking down the path that led to the pool house, her strawberry blonde ponytail swinging as wide as her hip swing.

"Get your sweet ass back here," I raced after her and grabbed her elbow. "I thought you came down here to see me? Sisters before misters, remember?"

Anna rolled her big blue eyes, but stopped in her tracks. "Okay, fine. But I'm not leaving here without meeting that guy."

I held my hands up like it didn't bother me at all that she wanted to eye-fuck my boyfriend. "Sure. Whatever. Let's go inside so I can change and then you can tell me what you're all doing here."

We all raced inside and I gave them a quick tour. All the girls in the sorority came from wealthy families, so my house wasn't super exciting for them. Plus, I didn't care to show off whatever my parents had purchased. It had nothing to do with me and my contribution to life. Not yet, at least.

When I'd pulled on a cute sundress and let one of the girls do my hair, I looked like I fit in with the group once again. "Anyone going to tell me what you're doing here?"

Natalie, the unofficial spokesperson of the group, leaned forward from her lounging position on my bed. "Ava tells us you are behind on your rush planning, which didn't sound like you at all, so we planned a little road trip to come see you. Pull you out of whatever funk you found yourself in that distracted you enough to neglect the sorority."

Well, that pissed me right off. "Wow. So Ava decided to spread some rumors—that aren't true, by the way—and you assumed I was in a funk?"

Courtney, the quiet one, spoke up. "Well, aren't you? We show up and you look like you've been working your fingers to the bone. I mean, girl, look at your ruined mani."

I looked down at my nails to see a few of them chipped, but I'd hardly call them ruined. Funny how one month could change your whole perspective when you weren't looking. A month ago I would have turned my nose up at chipped polish. Now, I figured there were more important things in life than a perfect mani/pedi.

"Let's go get some dinner and I'll fill you in on what's going on, huh?" I waved at the door to my bedroom to get them going. "There's a great little sushi place downtown I know you'll love."

As we filed out of the house, the whole group of us nearly ran into Lukas outside my front door. He was dressed in workout clothes, his hair adorably messed up. He glanced over the girls until he found me and then smiled, his eyes looking more at ease when they connected with mine.

"Hey. I take it our run is cancelled?" He glanced down at my dress and heels, the same outfit I'd worn the first night we met.

The girls all turned to look at me and I knew what they were thinking. Lukas already looked weary, like he wasn't sure who I was with these new people all around me. This was awkward.

"Um, yeah, sorry. We have dinner plans. I'll see you tomorrow though."

I hit the unlock button on my car keys and practically pushed the girls into it. I glanced back to see Lukas with a frown on his face, his jaw clenched like he was pissed. I couldn't blame him. I hadn't exactly been the nicest rushing off without introducing everyone.

"Bye, hottie motorcycle guy!" Natalie said out the window, fluttered her damn fingers at Lukas.

I threw it in drive and sped off, needing to put lots of space between my girls and my secret boyfriend. Having seen my friends in action at a frat party, I knew they only needed about ten seconds before they were able to turn a guy's head. Flirting was their superpower. Not that I thought Lukas would be that easily swayed, but why put that temptation out there, you know?

I dared a final glance in the rearview mirror and the sight nearly broke my heart. Lukas stood there by himself, staring after my car, his jaw hard as granite. The imposing stone facade of my house so counter to his casual T-shirt and shorts. His resting bitch face was back and this time it was directed at me.

$\sim$

"I seriously think the fresh air has gotten to your brain, D." Natalie kept stealing glances at me the whole time we ate dinner.

Little did she know it wasn't the fresh air. It was the small-town boy working for my father that had stolen all my attention. She was right. I was distracted by the churning in my stomach. I knew I hadn't handled things well back at home when Lukas came by and it didn't sit well with me. I just wanted to hurry up dinner and go talk to him. Which was crazy because I hadn't seen my friends in a whole month and normally I'd jump at the chance to spend time with them.

"Okay, let's focus, girls. We need to help Delta pick the main colors for bid week. That'll get Ava off her back." Anna, at least, was trying to help me.

I sighed while they all launched into an argument over the two best colors to convey their excitement over the new recruits. It all just seemed so trivial and shallow. Only a month ago I would have been arguing with them, just as excited by the prospect of a party, but now, it just didn't grab me. I wanted to talk about how I was making my software interface all pretty and ready to sell to the public. Maybe even chat about the possibility of falling in love at the tender age of twenty. The kind of stuff that made my heart pound.

"Hey, girls?" I asked quietly, the rest of them quieting down immediately.

The sounds of the restaurant faded into the background. I was going to break protocol and talk about something beyond parties, sororities, and the latest fashion. I wasn't at all sure how they'd take it, but they were my friends. I should be able to share my life with them.

"I wanted to tell you that I've been working on a side project and I'm really excited about it."

Natalie tipped her head to the side. "A new project?"

I nodded. "Yeah. I built some accounting software. And I think it's good enough to start selling it."

The silence stretched out while I fidgeted in my chair. This had been a bad idea. Sharing my programming with this audience was just stupid. What had I been thinking?

"Well, well. We have a boss bitch on our hands!" Natalie was the first to break the silence. "Congrats, girl. That sounds amazing. And confusing."

I giggled, relieved beyond belief that she supported me even though she probably didn't understand why I loved programming. The rest of the girls congratulated me and asked some questions about the software, which I answered, my heart glowing with pride. I'd underestimated these friends of mine and now I knew exactly what everyone else saw when they looked at me. I bet each of my friends had way more going on under the surface too, and when I went back to school, I intended to dig into what that was.

We also picked colors for bid week, sending that info off to Ava so she'd get off my back. The wait staff probably wanted us to leave so they could turn our table, but we all wanted to stay and catch up. I made a note to tip well to make up for hogging a table all evening. When we were just about to go, I decided to share one more thing with them.

"So, you know Lukas?" At their nods and Natalie's waggle of eyebrows, I continued. "We're kind of seeing each other."

"What?"

"Tell us!"

"I'm happy for you, Delta."

They all talked at once. I beamed, realizing I'd missed this. Having good friends to share everything with. Sure, Lukas and I were a team, but it wasn't us versus the world, like it seemed. I had girlfriends too who'd back me and not ask questions.

I swirled what was left of my ice water, buying time just to annoy them. "Well...we're keeping things a secret since he works for my dad, but he's pretty amazing."

My eyes filled with tears, surprising even myself. I hadn't truly realized what Lukas meant to me until this very moment. I'd never felt like someone's most important person. My parents had always had each other and the winery to take all their attention, and though I'd had good friends in high school and college, I'd never had a true bestie. Lukas and I felt like an extension of each other.

And I'd left him in my driveway by himself.

"Ahh, Delta," Anna oozed, leaning over to give me a hug.

I set down my glass and stood quickly. "Guys. I gotta get back and talk to Lukas."

"Okay, honey. Let's go." Natalie stood too and grabbed her purse.

Suddenly, there was nothing that mattered more than getting home and talking things out with Lukas. He needed to know me leaving him standing there hadn't been because I didn't think he was worthy of meeting my friends. It was because I was jealous and afraid they'd flirt with him and he'd dump me for someone prettier and new. I should have trusted him more, which meant I had some apologizing to do.

When my car pulled into my driveway, my friends yelled at me to go find Lukas while they got settled in our guest bedrooms. They'd be here through the weekend, which left plenty of time to talk. I threw them air kisses and ran as soon as my feet hit the ground. I flew down the path leading to the pool house and grabbed the door handle, only to find it locked. I knocked and then called out to him.

There was no answer. And no light on.

I went out back to the tree, thinking maybe he was working out, but there was no Lukas, no speaker, and no sign of him anywhere. I retraced my steps and realized in my race to find him, I'd missed the fact that his motorcycle was gone.

Oh, shit.

I spun in a circle, my hands in my hair.

He was gone.

9

Chapter 9

$\mathcal{L}$ukas

I wasn't the type to rage hot and fast, getting over it in the next breath. I stewed on things far longer than was healthy, letting it fester and build into something more than it was. And this little situation with Delta was no different. The second she dismissed me like the dust covering her fancy shoes in front of her girl-friends, I'd wanted nothing more than to get the hell out of Merlot.

Not seeing any other choice, I called in sick for the following day, and if truth be told, I was definitely feeling off. Seeing Delta shrug me off like that after I'd started to come to rely on her and think that maybe we really did have a chance together, put me in a permanent funk. I packed a small bag and hopped on my motorcycle to head home for the long weekend.

My parents, as conservative and as strict as they were growing up, were everything I needed to ground myself again. My dad was the town pastor and my mom was the stereotypical housewife. I didn't want to live my own life struggling to make ends meet like they did, but I had to admit, they had a fantastic marriage that had served my sister and me well throughout the years. Mom fed me heaping plates of all my favorites over the weekend and Dad even took the afternoon off on Saturday to have a family beach day.

My sister, Lenora, and her husband, Jayden, and their son, Red, met us down at the cliffs. Once their umbrella was pitched and Red had been slathered with enough sunscreen to stunt his growth, they settled down and joined the conversation. Their constant teasing and cajoling finally broke me out of my funk.

"So, now that you're speaking more than one word at a time again, want to tell us who the girl is?" Lenora shot me a look like she dared me to deny all this angst wasn't about a girl.

The thing is, Lenora looked all sweet and proper, but she ran a sex toy shop here in Auburn Hill and had the characteristics of a bulldog sniffing an unwatched cheeseburger. Denying my issue had to do with Delta wasn't an option. Better to just be out with it now.

"Her name is Delta and she's the daughter of my boss."

"Oh, son. Really know how to pick 'em," Dad muttered, his gaze firmly looking out at the sea. He didn't like conflict, what could I say?

Lenora whipped off her sunglasses. "Must run in the family, this attraction to bosses." She winked at my brother-in-law and I tried not to vomit. He'd been her boss for all of a day before he'd fired her. He apologized, of course, and then gave her the whole company right after he asked her to marry him.

"This is different though. Her family has owned this winery for decades. They're one of the wealthiest families in Merlot. They're not going to turn a blind eye to the poor guy renting their pool house for the summer dating their precious daughter."

Jayden sat up from where he was sunning on a beach towel. "I don't know, brother. If they can't see what a good guy you are, then maybe that's their issue, not yours. Do you love this girl?"

I ran a hand through my hair, uncomfortable with the question as it was the one that had been bouncing around in my skull all weekend long. *Was* I in love with her?

"Kind of feels like I am, but how do I know for sure?" I asked Jayden. He and my sister were nauseatingly happy together. If anyone could tell me, it would be him.

Jayden got a soft smile on his face, reaching over to hold Lenora's hand. "If you say something mean to her in the heat of the moment and it makes your throat burn to have said those things to her. Or if she winks at you and your heart stops beating. Or her laugh makes you feel higher than all the clouds in the sky. Or her eyes fill with tears and you'd literally do anything in the whole world to make her smile again. I'd have to say those are all indications that it's love."

Lenora made some sort of weird peep and then she was sitting on Jayden's lap, their lips smashed together. I groaned and my mom laughed. Dad's face turned a mottled red even though he never took his gaze off the ocean. Red, having seen this a lot, barreled right into them, wanting to be part of the huddle.

While they were occupied, I thought about what Jayden said. There was a lot of truth there, though it was Delta's dimples that had me on my knees. Biting her lip made me crazy. And I liked her conversation and presence even when getting naked wasn't on the menu. I even got that gushy feeling when I thought about her brain and how smart she was. If I was getting turned inside out over a girl's brain, it *had* to be love, right?

"Fuck," I muttered loudly.

"Lukas!" Mom chided.

"Sorry, Mom."

When Jayden and Lenora came up for air, Lenora turned her attention back to me. "Hey, don't let this get you down. You're a good man, Lukas Murphy. You deserve a good woman who can see through the zeroes on your bank account. And if you love her, you don't have to rush anything. Let everything run its course. You're young yet. Talk, be honest with each other, and just see what happens."

I stood up and ruffled her hair like when we were kids. I knew she hated it and it was just the thing a younger brother does. She slapped at my hands, but there was a smile on her face.

"Thanks, big sis. You're not so bad at this advice crap."

She grinned and smoothed down her hair. "Glad you think that. Because I'm going to need to be good at it."

We all looked at her in confusion. What was she getting at?

She looked at Jayden and he looked at her. At his nod, she exploded. "I'm finally pregnant!"

Mom nearly fell out of her chair getting to Lenora and pulling her into a joyous hug. Dad was slower, but he made it over there too. I gave Jayden a hug, not surprised to see tears in his eyes. He loved my sister better than I could ever have hoped for. I gave him some shit when he fired her, but he'd come around and redeemed himself.

"Congrats, Lenora." I gave her a hug once Mom finally let go. "You know Lukas is a really good name for a boy."

She punched me in the arm and then we just smiled at each other. Jayden pulled her against him and kissed the side of her head like she was his whole world, Red held in his other arm. Dammit, my eyes started burning too. See? This was what I wanted with Delta. A whole life built together.

I needed to get back to Merlot and see if she was on the same page. See if she was ashamed of me or if she simply didn't know what to do when two parts of her life came together unexpectedly.

The drive back early Monday morning was a good one. I'd left Merlot with anger thrumming through my veins. I was returning with cautious optimism. The way I saw it, I'd had the weekend to remember who I was. To solidify what I wanted in life. And if Delta wasn't the one for me, it would hurt to cut ties, but I'd do it because I knew what I ultimately wanted.

I headed straight to the winery, pulling up with exactly thirty seconds to spare before I was late for work. I ran in, grabbed an apron and got going on the dishes, ignoring Delta's staredown from the inventory job she was doing.

"When you're done there, Delta, let's have you work with Rosie in the tasting room." John swept through the back room. "Lukas, let's have you head over to the growers and get started on that side of things. You feeing better, by the way?"

I nodded, feeling guilty for calling in sick on Friday. Taking sick days was a rarity for me. "Yeah, I'm good. Thank you."

"Awesome. Have a good Monday, guys. Let me know if you need anything." John headed out to do all the other things he did besides manage the summer workers.

"You were sick on Friday?" Delta said across the room, the clipboard forgotten. "Was it bad? You didn't answer my texts."

"No, I'm okay, I promise. Maybe we can chat tonight after work?" I had a sink full of glasses that needed washing and I really wanted to get out to the field for the first time to learn that side of the business. Besides, our conversation might be a little intense and I needed more than a few stolen moments in the back room with her to say all the things I wanted to say.

She sighed, but nodded. "Okay. After work for sure. I'll meet you at the pool house?"

"Sure."

When her back turned and she resumed inventory, I took a long moment to drink her in. The way she kept pushing a piece of hair out of her face while she concentrated. Her checkered Vans that said more skater girl than sorority girl. I'd missed her while I was gone. And I hoped like hell she was falling for me just like I was falling for her.

~

I jiggled my keys in my hand while I waited for Delta. I was bursting with the knowledge I'd gained from working in the fields that day. My brain was in hyperdrive and a big part of me wanted to share it all with Delta, but we had to resolve things between us first.

She came out the back sliding door of her house, a pair of cut-off jean shorts and a skimpy red tank top that highlighted her bronzed skin. She had simple flip-flops on her feet, and though she looked nothing like the sorority girl I met that first night, I thought she looked even prettier just how she was. I remembered what Jayden said about loving someone and realized he'd been right. More than anything, I wanted to put a smile back on Delta's face.

"Hey, Lukas." She came to a stop in front of me, her hands twisting the little gold band rings around her fingers.

I hitched a thumb over my shoulder. "Want to go for a walk in the vineyard?"

She nodded, her expression looking nervous despite her casual words. "Sure!"

We headed out that way and I was aware of her beside me, her fruit scent tickling my nose. She stayed quiet until we got to the tree where I liked to work out. And then it was like she couldn't stop, the words pouring faster than a bottle of the reserve merlot they kept in the back for special customers.

"Listen, I'm so sorry for not introducing you to my friends and making things super awkward. It's just Natalie, the one with the big mouth, she's just so flirty and she said some things about you on your motorcycle and I just wanted to get them out of there. And then Anna was looking you up and down and I wanted to pull her damn hair until she screamed. I mean, I know you and I are a thing and you wouldn't have flirted back, but just the idea of them all over you made me a little crazy. So, I'm sorry."

I put my hand on her arm and stopped her. "It's okay. I get it now. I admit, I was hurt that you ran off so fast. Thought maybe you were ashamed to introduce me to your friends—"

"No! I promise—" Delta interrupted.

"But then I spent the weekend with my family and I squared things away in my head," I finished.

"And?" She looked so worried, like she had no idea how much I felt things for her. And yeah, I'd tossed around the L word over the weekend, and while it still scared the crap out of me to say it, it didn't make it any less true.

I tucked a hair behind her ear, drinking her in. "I'm in love with you, Delta."

She sucked in a huge breath of air, the inhale shaky and long. Then she burst into a smile and gasped, her dimples winking in the fading sunlight. "Oh, thank God! I mean, I love you too, Lukas."

She jumped into my arms and I caught her, spinning her around and almost taking out one of the grapevines. We both laughed and kissed, neither of us able to decide which we wanted to do more. I finally set her down on her feet and cupped her face.

"I know we can't be together like we want right now, but you need to know I'm all in. I'm into you in every way a man can love a woman. You got me? I want forever with you, even if we can't get started on it until after you graduate."

A tear slid down her cheek and I caught it with my thumb. She nodded while blinking back tears. "Ditto. To all that."

I grinned and then kissed her again, showing her exactly how much she meant to me. Most girls might think making out in a vineyard with the dirt and plants and insects a gross thing, but Delta had been raised on this land. It was her foundation, and she didn't mind spending time making out in the field while the sun set into the horizon behind us. When we finally pulled away, I grabbed her hand and we went on that walk together.

She laid her head on my shoulder as we walked. "I told my friends about my computer program."

"Bet they were proud of you."

She nodded. "They were. They think I'm a bit weird, but they were proud of me just the same. I judged them a bit harshly, thinking they were all about the parties and boys, but they really care for me beyond all that."

"Everyone deserves to have friends like that." I kissed the top of her head. "That's Dante for me. He's been my friend through thick and thin."

"I can't wait to meet him."

"And I can't wait to officially meet your friends," I reminded her.

She groaned.

"What? Too soon?" I teased her.

She poked me hard and we stopped to kiss because I couldn't seem to keep my hands off her.

Delta pulled back and asked, "Do you still see me as a spoiled rich girl?"

"Do you see me as a poor kid with no prospects?" I countered.

"No!"

"Same goes for me. I may have teased you about the sorority girl thing, but you're so much more than that, Delta. I've never met someone who I can share my every thought with. My hopes and dreams, and even my stupid ideas. And you amaze me every day with how much you know, what you can do when you set your mind to it. I'm so lucky to be with you, and though I don't say it enough, I hope you always know that."

Her hands gripped the bottom of my T-shirt, her eyes going from soft to firm in a matter of seconds. "We're going to make this work. You hear me, Lukas Murphy?"

I kissed her forehead. "We will. There are going to be bumps ahead, but we'll make this work. I promise."

We walked back to the pool house in the dark and Delta came inside.

Neither one of us saw her dad standing inside the glass door of the main house, his gaze locked on us.

10

 elta

"I better get home," I whispered against Lukas's skin.

His arms pulled me in tighter like he couldn't bear the idea of letting me go. My limbs felt sleepy as hell and I knew if I didn't get out of Lukas's bed, I would end up falling asleep and spending the night. Pretty sure my parents would have a shit fit if I didn't come home tonight. Twenty years old and still following my parents' archaic rules about curfews.

Lukas groaned, but he finally let me go and rolled away to pull some sweatpants on. The only reason I even got up was because I knew we had a whole lifetime to be together and my parents putting a stop to my college funds was not in the plan. It was that inspiring thought I kept in the forefront of my brain the whole time I got dressed and then headed to the front door. Lukas kissed me quick, his chest bare and his hair rumpled, looking entirely too yummy to say goodbye to. He opened the door for me and I stepped out, feeling him following me.

"Want to make sure you get home safe," he whispered, his voice already hoarse with sleep.

I smiled into the dark, loving that he was such a gentleman when my house was only twenty feet away. We took the short path to the pool area hand in hand, the moonlight guiding us. I stopped short and Lukas stopped a second after me.

My father sat in the lounge chair next to the pool.

In the dark.

With an empty wineglass in his hand.

"Daddy!" A deep dread replaced all the sleepy hope that had sedated my limbs this evening.

He pursed his lips and twirled the glass in his hand. "Someone care to tell me what the hell's going on under my own nose?"

Fuck. The secret appeared to be out now.

"Listen, Daddy. It's not—"

Lukas stepped forward and cut me off. "Sir, I'm in love with your daughter. Which I'm sure is not what you hired me for, but I won't apologize for it. She's amazing in so many ways, I couldn't *not* fall in love with her. I can promise you, though, nothing about loving Delta will interfere with my job."

My knees went weak, and if my father hadn't been sitting right there, I would have jumped on Lukas and begged him to take me back into that pool house where I could show him exactly how grateful I was for his support.

Daddy stood up abruptly, pulling my attention from Lukas. He swayed a second on his feet before righting himself. "You work for me. You live on my property. And now you're sleeping with my daughter?"

Lukas pulled himself up even straighter and looked at my father head-on. I needed to intervene before this thing got nasty.

"Daddy, stop." I put my hand out toward him. "I love Lukas. He treats me better than any boy I've dated. This is a good thing between us. Please don't ruin it."

Daddy glanced at me, his eyes softening slightly when they found me, but the pinch of his lips told me he was still extremely angry. I'd always toed the line, keeping any rebellions small and out of sight. He wasn't used to me standing up for myself and I wasn't exactly sure how this would go over.

He swung his head back to Lukas and pointed his finger at him. "When this summer job is over, so will this...thing...between you. Mark my words."

Daddy spun around and marched back toward the house, tossing over his shoulder, "Tick-tock."

Rage filled my chest. How dare he insinuate that what Lukas and I had was shallow and flimsy? He had no idea how I felt about this man who'd shown me more respect than my own family. Lukas listened to me. He saw every part of me and loved me for me. That was more than I could say for my own father. Daddy only loved me for what I could do for the company image.

The back door closed and the lights flipped off, plunging Lukas and me into darkness. He reached for me and I wrapped my arms around his neck, desperate for his touch.

"I'm so sorry, Delta," he whispered against my hair.

A lump lodged in my throat. I pulled back to look him in the eyes. "No. *I'm* sorry. I'm sorry my parents don't understand."

Lukas shrugged, but I could tell by the haunted look in his eyes he cared about their opinion very much. "I get it. I'm the hired help who preyed on their daughter's emotions."

I shook my head so hard I got dizzy. "You know that's not true. What they think about you and me changes nothing. We are a team, Lukas. We have a plan and we're going to follow through with it no matter what. And then, maybe, they'll understand. You're it for me."

He didn't waste a second claiming my lips and making me forget all about my father's judgements. Lukas made my heart melt and my body go up in flames. He challenged my brain and stimulated my creativity. How could something so right be wrong?

"Stay with me," he whispered against my lips.

I nodded, lost in the daze of his kiss, and he smiled. His fingers wrapped around mine and he tugged me back to the pool house. The sound of the night around us was comforting in its quietness. I didn't need fancy surroundings or the cushion of money to pave my way through life. All I really needed was Lukas.

When he shut the door behind us, I took the gold band off my middle finger. The ring I'd had since I turned sixteen. The ring that had been passed down from my great-grandfather's day, the one that had been in the family as a representation of how far we'd come. When my great-grandfather got married, all they could afford was a simple gold band. The winery had grown into a multimillion-dollar enterprise since then, but our roots came from a single grapevine.

"I want you to wear my ring." I held it out to Lukas, who looked down at it curiously. "My great-grandfather started this whole winery with nothing. And right now, you and I are at that nothing stage. We'll make it too, Lukas. You may be my daddy's backroom boy, but you're my everything. Never forget that."

His eyes went molten and I shivered. Lukas reached up and unclasped the gold chain around his neck and took the ring from me, stringing it onto the chain and putting it back around his neck.

"I'll wear it proudly. I'll work my ass off for us, Delta. You'll see."

His hands cupped my face. His jaw clenched with determination and I knew one day we'd talk about this night. The night we vowed things far more serious than wedding vows. This was a vow to never let the other person down and I meant it with every cell in my body. Lukas was everything good in my life.

I dropped to my knees and pulled him out of his sweatpants

before he could protest. I licked the tip of his cock, watching as he hardened before my eyes. Lukas growled at me, his eyes watching me hungrily. I put the full length of him in my mouth, pulling back slowly as he grew, my tongue flicking the tip. His taste flooded my mouth and I had to clench my thighs together to hold back my moan.

Lukas gathered my hair to the back of my head and pulled me back so that just the very end of his cock lay between my lips. Then he thrust into my mouth and he went all the way to the back of my throat. Tears gathered in my eyes, and I'd never been more turned on than in that moment, on my knees, choking on Lukas's cock. He kept thrusting, his control over me complete with the stranglehold he had on my hair. Spit dribbled down my chin while I tried to breathe through my nose. I was sure I looked a mess, but Lukas only seemed more turned on as he gazed down at me through slitted eyes.

He made a noise in his throat and pulled out of my mouth. I gasped in a lungful of air. Strong arms pulled me up and I wrapped my legs around his waist. Lukas carried me into the bedroom, dropping me onto the bed and stripping me of my shorts. He didn't waste any time, just plunged right into me with his pants around his ankles. He grunted and I moaned at the feel of him inside of me.

"Yes, yes, yes," I whispered, adjusting to the size of him.

He pumped once, then twice, before standing back up, his cock still in me. He looked crazed with want, his eyes half closed and his mouth slightly open. He reached between us and thrummed his thumb across my clit. I bucked at the strong zing of desire that rushed through my body, and he slid further in. He pulled back out and strummed again. It felt so good, but I really needed his cock filling me.

"Lukas, please," I begged.

The side of his mouth tilted up in a smile, a look I lodged in my brain so I'd always remember. He was half the sweet boy I knew and half a dirty man who knew how much he ruled my body.

His cock plunged all the way back in and my eyes rolled back in my head. Then he was out again, his thumb working me over. I writhed on the bed, my legs trying to pull him closer. I needed that cock more than I needed to breathe and Lukas was being a damn tease.

He used his free hand to pin my leg to the bed while he worked my clit. My breath started coming in short gasps and I knew I was about to come. He must have known too, because he notched his cock at my entrance and stroked back in. The second he filled me all the way, I came, my walls squeezing him tight. It felt so good it hurt, the waves of pleasure coming and coming, no end in sight.

Sometime later I heard him grunt and pull out. With my eyes squeezed shut, I whined, wishing he still filled me. Warmth hit my stomach and I fluttered my eyes open to see long, creamy ropes coating my stomach and breasts. Lukas shuddered above me, his strong arm bracketing my body. He reached down and dragged a finger across my breasts, making me quiver yet again. With heat still in his eyes, he put his finger to my lips. I opened and sucked his finger clean, tasting the tang of him and wishing I could taste him every single day for the rest of my life.

My ring, hanging from his chain, hung suspended between us. I knew, and I knew that he knew.

This was it.

Lukas and Delta.

Forever.

11

 ukas

I put my cell phone back in my pocket and turned toward the pool house. Delta would be home any minute now after going shopping for last-minute things she needed for the sorority house. We'd started a countdown that night her father found out about us. Summer had seemed long and endless when I'd first moved to Merlot for the job at Black Bishop Wineries, but now it had passed in the blink of an eye. Tomorrow, Delta left to go back to school and my job at Black Bishop ended.

Like Delta kept reminding me, this ending was really just a beginning for me and her.

And the phone call I'd just finished confirmed things were unfolding right on schedule.

"Hey, babe!" Delta came bounding down the path to the pool house, multiple shopping bags in hand.

Everything in me relaxed at the sight of her dimples and

broad smile. It was like my personality had been born grumpy, but she made the sun come out just by being around. I'd miss her when she left. And that ache would make me work that much harder to bring our dream to fruition, just so she'd come back to me with that grin and twinkle in her eyes. What had started out as a dream to make something of myself, now had become a joint dream, one where if we weren't together, the rest didn't matter. I wanted it all now: the winery, the success, and most of all, Delta.

"Hey. Did you get what you needed?" I snagged a quick kiss before opening the door so she could put her bags down inside. She'd more or less moved into the pool house the last few weeks, irritating her parents even more, though they hadn't retaliated or tried to forbid her from seeing me.

"I did." She spun and threw her arms around my neck, stretching up to kiss me like she'd missed me too, even if she'd only been gone an hour.

"I've got news," I said against her lips.

Her eyes lit up. "You're going to stow away in my suitcase and live in the sorority with me?"

My mouth hitched up on the side. "Um, no, thanks. Living with a bunch of sorority girls?" I shuddered at the thought.

Delta smacked me on the arm. "Hey, watch it, mister. I'm a sorority girl too and you like me just fine."

"Mmm, I sure do." I nuzzled into her hair and kissed my way down her neck.

"Focus, Lukas." Delta tried to be demanding, but ruined it by ending her demand with a little moan.

I chuckled and backed off enough to tell her the news. "I just got off the phone with Jordan Rhoades. He owns that little winery called Easy Rhoades. He needs a vineyard manager and is willing to take a chance on me. I just accepted the job for the busy fall season. I start Monday."

Delta jumped up and down and then smothered me in a hug, peppering kisses all over my face. "I'm so happy! I knew you'd find something, Lukas. Oh my God! It's really truly happening, isn't it?"

Nodding, my heart pounded away at the realization that we were onto the next step in our grand plan. "Yeah, it really is."

"Well, I've got news too." Delta winked at me, biting her lip.

I tilted my head and waited, knowing it had to be good based on the way her eyes sparkled in the afternoon sunshine.

"I just got the email from the counseling department that they've officially declared my major as business!" Delta looked ready to burst with excitement.

She jumped and I caught her, pulling her into my chest and spinning her around in a circle. She did it. She'd declared her major so she'd be poised to help us set up the business side of our dream. I'd learn how to make the wine, she'd learn how to sell it. A dream team.

I set her down and held her beautiful face in my hands. "We're doing it, baby."

Her eyes went soft on the edges. "You and me."

"Forever," I whispered right before sealing our lips together in an indecent kiss. Time spun away, leaving just the two of us in our own little world. Having a dream was so much better when it was shared with someone else. I didn't believe in soul mates prior to this summer, but my trip to Merlot had opened my eyes to so much more.

A loud wolf whistle interrupted us. We both looked over to see Delta's sorority girls standing on the path by the pool, grinning and making googly-eyed faces. My stomach swooped, realizing my time with Delta had come to an end. Plus, a small part of me wondered if she'd ignore me now that her girls were here.

I shouldn't have worried though, as Delta laced our fingers together and walked us over to her friends.

"Girls, this is Lukas, my boyfriend. Lukas, these are the girls. Natalie, Blair, Bree, Courtney, and Anna." Delta introduced us.

A simple hand lift was all I managed before they swarmed

me, shouting out questions and blocking my view of Delta. A cloud of perfume choked my throat and I'd never felt more claustrophobic.

Another loud whistle broke it up, Delta pushing her way back toward me. "Girls! Step off my man!"

Thankfully, they did step back, giving me room to breathe and to tug Delta back to my side, my arm over her shoulder. She laid her head on my shoulder like she knew just how much I didn't want to be surrounded by a gaggle of girls. I was a one-woman man.

"It's nice to meet you, ladies." I gave them a head nod.

"Oh, we've heard all about you, Lukas. Nobody has made Delta smile like that." Natalie pointed to Delta's beaming face.

I looked down at Delta as she peered up at me. I could get lost in that face for hours at a time.

"Oh my God, you two are adorable," Bree sing-singed, her hands clasped under her chin.

"I hate to break the bad news, but we've gotta get Delta's things packed in the car and head out. There's a sorority meeting tonight to prepare for rush week," Anna said softly, looking like she'd personally scheduled that meeting and had to apologize.

Delta's eyes turned worried and I spun her in front of me, her breasts smashed against my stomach. Running a thumb under her chin, I tilted her face up to me.

"Hey. This isn't goodbye. This is just a temporary thing to get us to where we want to be. Remember?"

Her eyes filled with tears anyway, and my heart lurched in my chest.

"I know." She nodded, but didn't look convinced. "New rule? We talk every single day?"

I smiled gently. "You bet. Not a day goes by we don't talk." I pulled the chain and ring out from under my shirt. "We're already starting with so much more than nothing. Let's build something great."

Delta grabbed the back of my neck and brought me down so she could kiss me. Her tongue swept my lips and I let her in. Friends watching be damned. If my girl wanted to claim me in front of anyone, including her parents, I'd let her. Knowing she wasn't ashamed of me made me feel like more of a man than turning eighteen had.

A throat clearing had us breaking apart. Out of the corner of my eye, I could see her parents coming out the back door and skirting the pool. Delta gave me a stern look, which I knew meant to keep my emotions in check. Her parents weren't exactly supportive of us dating, but I couldn't let their judgement color our decisions.

"All ready to head out?" Mr. Bishop said gruffly.

Delta's mom rushed forward and gave her a hug. "Straight A's now. Like we talked about. Next summer we'll have your father train you to take over the management of the tasting room."

Bitterness filled my veins listening to Delta's mom give her instructions instead of simply telling her she loved her. What mother sends her kid off with business instructions instead of a simple I love you and I'll miss you? Delta didn't seem phased by it. She just nodded and pasted on a fake smile. I vowed to give her all the love and acceptance her parents didn't.

Mr. Bishop gave her a quick pat on the back and then marched back inside without even giving me a glance. Typical and expected. I didn't hope for more. He'd always see me as the backroom boy renting his pool house, not the man who'd give his daughter everything she ever wanted.

Once her parents left, I helped Delta move her suitcases into the back of her car. Her friends argued over who would drive with who as they caravanned to campus. When Delta was busy fitting another bag into the car, I pulled Natalie aside. Despite her obvious flirty nature, she remained serious, like she knew I wasn't up for joking.

"Hey. Promise me you'll look out for her. If she's having any problems, you'll call me?" I handed her a Black Bishop business card with my name and cell number on it.

She took it, tucking it in her back pocket and giving me a genuine smile. "I promise you. She'll be fine, but if not, you'll be the first to know. I'm just glad to see Delta so happy. You're good for her, Lukas, so you're all good in my book."

"Thank you." I rushed back to Delta's side, not wanting to miss a second when we had so few left.

She shut the trunk and dusted off her hands. I could feel the sense of dread pouring off her in waves.

"Hey." My hands settled on her hips and pulled her close. "You can come home and see me anytime. You're just a short drive away. This isn't a goodbye that leads to sadness. This is just a time for us to go after our dream. Together. No amount of miles can separate us."

She nodded despite the tears in her eyes. "I know. I'm just so damn impatient to start that part of our lives now."

I kissed her quick. "All in good time."

Without wasting another second, I pulled a ring out of my back pocket and held it out to her. The shiny gold reflected the sun. She glanced down at it and then back up at me.

"What's this?"

"It's our own start. And it's my promise to you. We may be starting with very little, but I promise to give you everything."

Delta leaped into my arms, the ring crushed between us. "You already have, handsome."

Eventually, I got to slide the ring on, a tear or two tracking down her cheeks. It was a perfect fit on her left ring finger. The perfect promise of our bright future. Her friends finally got restless and nagged her to get going, interrupting our moment. I didn't blame them. I could have spent days out here saying goodbye to Delta and still not be ready.

I gave her one last kiss, memorizing the feel of her lips against mine, the way her body's curves fit tucked against mine. And then she climbed in her car, shut the door, started the engine, and rolled down the window.

With a tear spilling over, she smiled so big her dimples popped out.

"See you later, alligator," she hollered out the window.

"In a while, crocodile," I said right back, waving like the lovesick guy I'd become until her car was out of sight.

Time to put our plan in motion and get to work on building a life worthy of Delta. Because once I'd done that, I could slide another ring on her finger and make her mine forever.

EPILOGUE

$\mathcal{L}$ukas

Two years later - Auburn Hill, CA

"You look amazing." I could barely get the words out of my mouth, seeing Delta sashay her way into the small tasting room.

Her red dress fluttered on her tanned thighs, the top part fitted to her curves like a second skin. She'd been growing out her blonde hair, teasing that she wanted me to have plenty to wrap around my fist when we made love. She teased me a lot the last two years while she was away at college. Flirty texts, mailed love letters, sexy video chats with very little clothing involved, and the occasional surprise visit when she just couldn't stay away.

Two years had done nothing to dampen our youthful infatuation. In fact, our love had only grown deeper. Stronger. The kind that could last a lifetime and beyond.

Much to her parents' disappointment.

We'd invited them to our opening-day ceremony, but they'd declined, saying they had a prior commitment. I knew their response hurt Delta and I despised them for it. How could they not see what an amazing woman she'd become? How could they not want to celebrate her accomplishments?

Delta twirled in a circle and I forgot about everything else. Her dress dropped to a steep V in the back, leaving her silky skin bare. I clenched my jaw and realized I'd have to work hard all day to keep my focus on our opening ceremonies when all I really wanted was to strip Delta down to her high heels and touch every inch of her body.

"You keep looking at me like that and we'll be late to our own party," she murmured, coming close enough I could drag my hands up her arms.

"You keep wearing dresses like that and we'll never leave this place," I answered back, my nerves at an all-time high.

Today was the fulfillment of our dream. The opening of our tasting room, which Delta knew about. Tomorrow, we'd plant the first field of grapevines in the plot of land behind us that we'd just purchased which would produce our first estate-bottled wines. What Delta didn't know about was the diamond ring I intended to slide on her finger tomorrow. Yeah, we were still young at twenty-two to be getting married, but we'd waited long enough for our dreams. It was time to start living them.

"Let's go before you ruin my dress or my carefully applied makeup." She gave me a saucy wink and wrapped herself around my arm, reminding me of the first night I'd met her, walking home drunk by herself.

I'd never been more proud to have Delta on my arm. We walked across the new oak floors my friend, Titus Jackson, had put in recently. The whole build-out of the tasting room had gone surprisingly smooth, but then again, using contractors you'd grown up with usually meant they wouldn't screw you over. Living and working in my hometown fulfilled something deep inside of me I couldn't quite describe.

We exited the heavy wooden door to squint our eyes in the midday sunlight as we stood on the expansive porch. A soft gasp came from Delta's mouth. There before us on the small patch of grass stood a crowd of Auburn Hill citizens. I spotted Dante, who gave me a head nod of congratulations, my parents, my sister and her husband and kids, many of the people I'd gone to high school with, even my old math teacher and the gossip-loving town mail carrier.

A car door slammed and footsteps crunched over the gravel parking lot as another couple approached. Delta gasped again and I looked over to see her parents joining the party. A little spot of hope bloomed in my chest and dialed the nerves up another notch.

The circle of California winemakers was a small one. Everyone knew everyone else. After my summer working for Mr. Bishop, he hadn't exactly been warm and friendly, but he also hadn't gone out of his way to make it hard for me to work my way into the circle. In fact, he'd been the one to introduce me to the grower we currently bought our grapes from. I owed him a great deal professionally, and certainly personally, for giving me the love of my life.

I wrapped my fingers around Delta's and stood tall. "Thank you all for coming here today. River Delta Wineries welcomes you today and every day going forward. We have a full tasting prepared for you, so come on in."

One by one, the group came into the tasting room, where Delta poured efficiently, all the while answering questions and walking everyone through the flavors of our first batch of wines. I helped her pour, feeling only slightly awkward being front and center. The tasting room was Delta's stage. I liked being in the background making the wines, but for opening day, I'd do whatever was necessary.

Nearing the end of the two-hour opening, we'd sold almost half our inventory of wine bottles already. If we kept up at a normal pace after today, we'd need to dramatically increase our quantity of wine for next year to keep up.

Mr. Bishop clapped me on the shoulder. "Well done, Lukas. The varietals don't taste like a first run."

High praise indeed from a guy who owned a winery that had been around for almost a hundred years.

"Thank you, sir."

He put his hand out and I shook it, both our grips firm. Something crazy ran through my head, and unlike me, I jumped at the idea without thinking it through.

"Can I talk to you privately for a moment?"

Mr. Bishop frowned, but nodded. He walked with me to the back room where the used glasses had stacked up by the industrial sink. Here I was, the owner of a winery, and I knew I'd still be the one doing the dishes later that night. It did not escape my notice that I was once again the backroom boy as I asked for Mr. Bishop's acceptance of me asking Delta to marry me.

"I intend to give Delta an engagement ring tomorrow. I'm not asking your permission as I don't feel Delta would want that. But I am asking for your acceptance of our marriage. It would mean a great deal to Delta, and therefore to me, that you and your wife accept our relationship."

Mr. Bishop didn't move, his frown frozen in place. I was just about to concede that he would never accept me when he finally answered.

"It's not what I had planned for Delta, but even I can see that you're a good man and will give her a good life. Maybe later when River Delta is firmly established, we can discuss you and Delta also taking the reins of Black Bishop. It's her birthright and now yours, as her husband if she says yes."

My brain blanked out. Was he saying he'd one day give the winery to us? He trusted Delta and me enough to give away his family's winery? All I could think about was Delta's face when she heard her father trusted her with her birthright.

I stuck out my hand, my throat closed too tight to speak. Mr. Bishop shook it, all the while staring me down. He could stare all he wanted. I wasn't intimidated. I was already living my dream with the love of my life.

∼

Delta

"Holy shit, I'm exhausted!"

Every muscle in my body ached, but it was a delicious pain. The type that told me I'd done an honest day's work alongside my boyfriend. I'd take manual labor over boring classes any day of the week, especially after the success of our opening yesterday. Which was good because we still had a long way to go to get this field planted.

Lukas had been right last year when he'd bought the land for the tasting room. He knew the land behind it would eventually go for sale when the owner passed away and it was the perfect spot for grapes. Little bit of sun, little bit of shade, lots of ocean breeze and gentle hills.

"Come here," Lukas wrapped me up in his arms, all sweaty and dirty, just like me.

"Ew! We're stinky!" I huffed.

"Don't go sorority girl on me, woman," he teased, knowing all too well how I'd shown him the true strength of a sorority girl. "Seriously though. Come over here. I have a surprise for you."

He tugged me toward the huge oak tree on the far side of the property line. "I called in a few favors from my sister and her gaggle of friends she calls the Hell Raisers. You remember meeting them? They still live up to their name, even though they're all moms with minivans and diaper bags now."

I did remember meeting them. They were pretty badass in the way they welcomed other women into their group and had each other's backs. I was hoping to find the same type of friends now that I lived in Auburn Hill.

We crested the slight hill and I saw a whole picnic laid out under the tree. A red-checked blanket, a basket, and a battery-operated lantern. My heart squeezed, seeing the effort Lukas went to, the sight a reminder of our first date when he'd made the same picnic in Merlot. I hoped this date ended the same way that one had. My insides went molten at the thought, dirt-covered skin be damned.

We sat and ate, enjoying the shade and the chance to relax. We went over sales from yesterday and discussed our harvesting goals. Then I forgot all about the winery when Lukas stood up, his eyes an intense dark blue. Finally, the part of this date I'd been hoping for as dessert.

But then I was confused. Instead of stripping like I assumed, he reached into his back pocket and then knelt on one knee. I sat straight up and sucked in air that had gone thin on me.

"Delta Bishop. I've loved you near and far. I've loved you when I didn't want to and when I probably shouldn't have. I've loved you when we were young and I promise to love you when we're old. My dream was always a winery, but I had no idea the real dream was you. Will you do me the honor of being my wife?" His eyes were shiny, but his jaw was firm.

Lukas held out a stunning diamond ring I knew we couldn't afford in the palm of his dirty hand. My whole body shook and his words buzzed in circles in my head. My throat decided to seize and I had to gulp repeatedly to clear it.

"Yes. Yes, I'll marry you!" I said the moment I could get the words out.

I scrambled to my feet and Lukas grabbed my hand to slide the ring on my finger. The second it was on, I jumped, tackling him and tumbling us both to the blanket. His grin and the unfamiliar weight on my finger made my heart soar to impossible heights. How could one girl be so damn happy? I peppered his face with kisses until he rolled us over and took charge.

Somehow our clothes found a new home in the dirt, our bodies like two magnets coming together by a force much stronger than we could deny. He filled me so completely I knew I could never breathe a day without Lukas on this earth. He was part of me and I was part of him. He whispered all kinds of things in my ear, some filthy, some sweet. But most of all, we whispered our love for each other, painting our land with a foundation strong enough for generations to come.

He may have started out as the backroom boy, but Lukas would always be front and center to me.

Want to read more about Lukas's sister, Lenora? Start with the first book in the Jobs From Hell series, Love Bank, and get all the craziness of love in a small town!!

Don't forget to download the FREE novella, Man Glitter! All that sawdust in every muscled crevice of my half-naked neighbor looks like man glitter when he handles his wood...

ACKNOWLEDGMENTS

I hope you enjoyed Backroom Boy, part of the shared world of the
All American Boy Series.
Want to read all of them?
Find them here on Kindle Unlimited:

Sierra Hill *The Boy Next Door*
Poppy Parkes *Boy Toy*
Evan Grace *The Boy Scout*
Emily Robertson *The Boyfriend Hoax*
Kaylee Ryan and Lacey Black *Boy Trouble*
Kimberly Readnour *Celebrity Playboy*
Marika Ray *Backroom Boy*
Leslie McAdam *Boy on a Train*
KL Humphreys *Bad Boy*
Nicole Richard *Hometown Boy*
Remy Blake *That Boy*
Stephanie Browning *The Boy She Left Behind*
Stephanie Kay *About a Boy*
Renee Harless *Lover Boy*
SL Sterling *Saviour Boy*

Special thanks to Jo-Anna Walker for the incredible Cover Design. Thanks to Judy Zweifel for cleaning this book up and trying to teach me how to use a hyphen appropriately.
To my Rays of Sunshine: you give me life. <3

ALSO BY MARIKA RAY

ABOUT THE AUTHOR

Marika Ray is a USA Today bestselling author, writing steamy RomCom and sweet romances to make your heart explode and bring a smile to your face. All her books come with a money-back guarantee that you'll smile at least once with every book.

If you'd like to know more about Marika or the other novels she's currently writing, please find her on Facebook, or her private Reader Group. Or you can find her in-person, on the beach in Southern California, frolicking like a Baywatch babe.

If you want to take your stalking to the next level, here are other legal places you can find Marika:

Join her Newsletter -
http://bit.ly/MarikaRayNews

Amazon - https://www.amazon.com/author/marikaray

Goodreads -
https://www.goodreads.com/author/show/16856659.Marika_Ray

Bookbub - https://www.bookbub.com/authors/marika-ray

Made in the USA
Middletown, DE
23 July 2023